BOYSTOWN 13

Fade Out

MARSHALL THORNTON

Published by Kenmore Books

Edited by Joan Martinelli

Cover design by Marshall Thornton

Images by 123rf stock

ISBN-13: 9798603507361

First Edition

❀ Created with Vellum

I'd like to thank Joan Martinelli, Nathan Bay, Kevin E. Davis, Helene Augustyniak, Robin Sinclair, Valerie and Randy Trumbull, and The Chicago Tribune Archives.

Chapter One

BERT HARKER BOUGHT ME A SOFA. Four years ago.

It was covered in a knobby, beige, fire-retardant fabric that on close inspection resembled spun plastic. The design was boxy and bland, not meant to be the focal point in anyone's living room. It was designed to disappear under an Erté print or behind a lacquered Oriental coffee table or at very least melt away next to an expensive entertainment center.

That was the designer's plan, but in my apartments the sofa had always been the main attraction. There was no competition from the director's chairs or the industrial shelves that held my electronics or my dinged-up metal desk or the tiny dining table in front of my window. As far as furniture went, the sofa was the star.

I hadn't liked it at first. Hadn't wanted it. But I'd slowly become accustomed to it. I'd recovered from broken bones and beatings on it, I'd fucked on it, I'd grieved on it; my lover, Harker, spent time dying on it, and so did my friend Ross.

The arms had turned from beige to gray; the cushions were now stained with red wine, coffee, soup, Hawaiian Punch and in one spot blood—I have no idea from which wound or for that matter even whose blood it was. There were at least three cigarette burns and one actual tear. Most of the time, to keep from having to buy another sofa, I covered it with an old afghan.

Really, it was time to let it go, to drag it out of the building and leave it in an alley for someone to pick it up and find a new life for it. Its time with me was done, but somehow I wasn't ready to admit that. So it sat in my living room, dirty, dilapidated and a little smelly.

I was sitting on it when the police showed up and began banging on my door. It was early on the last day of July. My lover Joseph had left me a day or two before. My friend Ross was dying in a hospital nearby. Even though I had no idea why the police were there, it made perfect sense that they would be out in the hallway threatening to break the door down.

Without deciding to, I got up off the sofa and answered the door. A detective I didn't know stood there with a couple of uniforms. He said, "Nick Nowak, I'm arresting you for the first-degree murder of Rita Lindquist."

"Really? That's interesting."

"Interesting? You think it's *interesting*?"

I shrugged. I did find it interesting that Rita was dead, that someone had gotten the upper hand on her. I mean, she'd never struck me as the victim type. The detective was a bit younger than me and either Italian or Mexican, I couldn't tell. He recited my Miranda rights to me and asked if I understood them.

I shook my head and said, "No."

"Don't be a smart ass." He pushed past me saying, "We have to search the apartment." The uniforms followed him inside.

It crossed my mind to ask to see a search warrant, but I didn't. Technically, they could look around to make sure I didn't have any weapons or evidence I might destroy. I did have a Sig Sauer and a Baby Browning. I said a mental fond farewell to each. One of the uniforms grabbed me by the wrists and cuffed my hands behind my back.

Disconnected. I felt disconnected from the things that were happening. It was as though I were watching myself on TV, as though I'd just tuned in and this was all part of some show I didn't know the name of and was just as clueless about the plot.

"Which district are you from?" I asked the detective.

"Town Hall."

"Where's Hamish?"

Hamish Gardner was the detective I knew there. The guy I'd dealt with from time to time. I didn't like him much and he certainly didn't like me. Still, at a moment like this his unfriendly face would have been appreciated.

"Detective Gardner is at your office. Where the body was found."

"Rita's body was found at my office?" That didn't make sense. None of this made sense, of course, but Rita's body being found at my office made the least sense of all.

The detective didn't answer my question just gave me a look that said I should know the answer to that.

"And who are you?" I asked.

"Detective Tim Burke." His name sounded a lot like timber, which I'd bet was his nickname all through grade school. I looked into his eyes. Reading my mind, he said, "You make a crack about my name and I'll beat the shit out of you."

"Nice to meet you, Detective Burke."

To the uniform holding onto my arm, he said, "Take him downstairs, put him in the back of a squad."

I was led out of my apartment and down the hallway to the elevator. A couple of neighbors were standing in their doorways watching what was happening. I had no idea there were so many people at home on a weekday morning. Glad I could entertain them.

At the elevator, the uniform pressed the down button. I glanced at his chest. His name tag said PATTOn. He wasn't that tall, had sandy brown hair and a pronounced underbite. At another point in my life I'd have been trying to figure out how to get him to suck me off in the elevator, murder charge or no murder charge.

"What the fuck are you looking at?" he demanded. Apparently, I'd been staring.

"Nothing."

The elevator door opened and he shoved me inside. I slumped

against the back wall and made a half-assed attempt to figure out what was going on. Rita Lindquist. Dead. Okay. So who killed her? And why did the police think it was me? Wait, that part was easy. She was killed in my office. That's what Timber had said, right? So all I needed to do was figure out who wanted Rita dead and who'd think killing her in my office was a great idea. At the intersection of those two ideas would be the killer.

Unfortunately, no one came to mind. There were definitely people in the world who'd want to kill Rita. I could easily name a few of them. But I couldn't think of anyone who would *also* want to do it in my office.

We reached the first floor. As we left the elevator, I asked, "How?"

"What?"

"How was Rita killed?"

"Cute. Really cute."

"I think I have a right to know."

"You already know. So cut the shit."

At Two Towers, the buildings were joined by a glassed-in walkway. Halfway down were doors that opened onto the circular drive. The office was in the south building, and as Patton and I got close to the front door the manager of my building—a tall, awkward girl named Clementine—rushed over, saying, "Nick what's happening? Where are they taking you?"

"None of you your business, ma'am," Patton said.

"Nick, do you need me to call someone for you? A lawyer?"

"I'll be fine," I said, right before Patton pushed me out the front door.

"Nick!"

Moments later, I was crushed into the back of a blue-and-white. The doors locked instantly, and did not have the luxury of inside handles. Patton walked away—to argue with Clementine, I think—leaving me sliding around on the vinyl seat with my hands uncomfortably cuffed behind me.

Well, this was a pretty picture. Me in the back of a squad.

Lights unnecessarily flashing. Every few minutes someone would come out of the building: An old woman walking a tiny little dog; a young banker heading down to the Loop; a scrawny old queen I've seen at the bars. They all stared at me and then quickly looked away.

Half of me was trying to figure out how to get more information. If I knew what happened to Rita it would be easier to make them understand I didn't kill her. And the other half, well, that half didn't give a shit. Lock me up, throw away the key. Fine by me.

Ten minutes later, Patton came back and got into the car. I couldn't resist saying, "Home, James." Like he was chauffeuring me. That went over like a lead balloon.

We drove down the Inner Drive to Addison, then turned west. Town Hall station was on the corner of Addison and Clark. An old two-story brick building that I'd been to many times, though never like this.

Patton pulled around the back, got out, and hustled me into the station though a rear entrance. He took the cuffs off and handed me over to a middle-aged man who was civilian support. He'd been sitting at an old wooden desk devoting all his attention to smoking a cigarette. He was quite good at it, and I could tell it annoyed him to be interrupted.

Reluctantly, he got out a fingerprint card and asked me a bunch of questions with about as much emotion as the default message on an answering machine.

"Name?"

"Nick Nowak."

"Nicholas?"

"Sure." It said Mikolaj on my birth certificate but same difference.

"Middle name?"

"Dawid."

The guy looked up at me.

"David."

"Address?"

I rattled it off. "3220 Lake Shore Drive apartment 1008, Chicago, 60657."

"Employer?"

"Me."

"Employer's address?"

"3257 Clark, Chicago, 60657."

"North Clark?"

"Yes."

"Social?"

I was tempted to say, "Very," but gave him my social security number instead.

"Date of birth?"

"April 25, 1948."

"Place of birth?"

"Chicago."

"Sex?"

"You're not my type."

He gave me another look and then put an M in that box. For good measure he put a C in the box for race. Caucasian.

"Height?"

"Six foot three."

"Weight?"

"One ninety. After a big meal."

He must have been getting tired of me because he gave me another glance and filled in the boxes for hair and eyes with two B's. My eyes are actually hazel, but I decided not to quibble.

That was all he needed. With a nod he let me know I should sit at the chair next to his desk and he got out an ink pad. He moved his chair over close to mine and then took my right hand. One by one, he rolled my fingers on the ink pad and then on the card.

He was close to me. Closer than I liked. He smelled of stale cigarette smoke, sweat and drugstore aftershave. I can't say I was enjoying the intimacy of being arrested. It took an excruciatingly long time to finish rolling my fingers on the card. When he was finally done, he made me sign the card, then handed me a tissue so I could rub the ink around on my fingertips.

Then he got up and led me over to a little setup where they took mug shots. It was a lot like the DMV, except not as much fun. I just stood there and let it happen. I didn't know what kind of face to make. I mean, should I smile, frown, look sad? I didn't have a 'you've been falsely accused of murder' face and I couldn't guess what it would look like anyway.

After we were done with the photo, the guy—who didn't have a name tag and hadn't bothered to introduce himself—led me back to his desk. He took out a big plastic bag and a receipt book. He handed me the bag.

"Shoelaces, belt, keys, wallet, anything else in your pockets. Anything else not in your pockets. I'm going to write down everything and give you a receipt to sign. Don't try to keep anything. If they find it later on you'll probably never see it again. This is your chance to protect your valuables. I suggest you take it."

I began giving him my stuff. The laces to my Reeboks, I wasn't wearing a belt, my keys, my wallet which was crammed full with a lot of stuff—none of it money—a wad of cash from my pocket, some change, my beeper, receipts I was going to expense to the job I'd finished the week before.

"Forty-three dollars, fifty-four cents," Mr. Smiley said after he counted my money. "I'm going to turn the beeper off so it doesn't lose its charge."

That seemed considerate until I remembered that they could probably search it and would need it to be nice and charged for that. When I was done handing him things, he held out the receipt and said, "Read it. If you agree, sign at the bottom then rip off the pink copy and put it in the bag."

I looked it over. It seemed okay. I signed. Meanwhile, Smiley had picked up his phone and dialed an internal number.

"The package is ready."

It was hardly a secret that I was the package and I don't think I was being called that so I wouldn't know what was going on. He was deliberately telling me I wasn't human. That I was just a thing to be passed around the station. My humanity had been checked at the door.

7

Patton came back and led me out of that area and up a flight of stairs to the second floor. Now I was in familiar territory. There were two interview rooms in the back of the floor. I'd been in each of them at least once.

Windowless. A metal table. A couple of metal chairs. Patton pushed me in and said, "Make yourself comfortable." As though that were even a possibility.

Then I waited.

Chapter Two

A LITTLE MORE THAN an hour later, Hamish Gardner came into the airless room. He was in his mid-forties and looked like he could use a couple years of sleep. He held a Styrofoam cup of coffee in one hand and a manila folder already thick with paper in the other. He looked at the room and said, "Stuffy in here, isn't it?"

"Open a window," I suggested.

He smiled. "You want a sandwich? It's kind of gross. Bologna."

I shook my head.

"Well let's see if we can get you out of here quickly."

Sitting down across from me, he opened the folder and pretended to read the top sheet. "In your own words tell me why you killed Rita Lindquist."

I didn't have any words that were even remotely related to Rita's death so I didn't say anything.

"Fuck. I almost forgot." He flipped through the folder and pulled out a sheet. "You've been read your rights. If you want to waive them you need to sign here."

I stared at the paper.

"You can have a lawyer if you want, but we both know he's not going to let you talk to me."

That was the smart thing to do. Keep my mouth shut. And

honestly, I didn't have a whole lot to say. But I wanted to know what Gardner had to say. It was Wednesday, or maybe it was Thursday. I wasn't even sure. Either way, they could hold me about seventy-two hours, which took us to at least Saturday. There was no court on Saturday, so I was clearly not getting to bond court until Monday morning. I didn't much like the idea of not knowing anything about why I was being accused of murder until Monday morning.

I signed the sheet of paper.

"Good boy," Hamish said, wearing the kind of smile you usually see on a used car salesman right after he'd sold you a car with a cracked engine block.

"All right then, let's get started. Rita Lindquist shot you, didn't she? Back in December?"

"Yes. That's true."

"Fucking bitch." That was Hamish establishing rapport. Didn't work.

"I didn't take it personally."

"A woman shot me, I'd hate the cunt. I'd want to get back at her."

"Well, that's you, isn't it? I think Rita hated me a lot more than I hated her." The last part was a hundred percent true.

"Yeah, the problem with that is she's dead and you're not."

"When was Rita killed?"

"Why don't you tell me," he suggested. "I bet you've got a better idea."

"You don't know when she was killed?"

"We're narrowing it down. Right now it's sometime between eleven Saturday night and eleven Sunday morning. Where were you during those hours?"

"Asleep," I said. That wasn't good and I knew it. But it wasn't a good idea to make up an alibi.

"Alone?"

"Probably."

"You're shitting me. You don't know if you were alone?"

"I drank a bunch of NyQuil. Slept for about twelve hours. I

was alone when I got in bed and I was alone when I got out. I couldn't tell you what happened in between. "

That was true. Joseph might have come home and slept a few hours next to me. I had no idea. Or maybe he came home and grabbed a few things and went out again. That was also possible. Unlikely, but possible.

"What kind of bullshit is that?"

"My friend is in the hospital. When I left there my boyfriend stayed. He might have come back to the apartment. I don't know. He wasn't there when I woke up."

"So your boyfriend lives with you?"

"Not anymore."

"You just said he might have come home Saturday night. That implies—"

"He left me on Monday."

"Because you killed Rita Lindquist?"

"No."

"Really? He wouldn't mind living with a murderer?"

I just stared at him.

"Why'd he dump your ass then?"

"None of your business."

"How do I get a hold of this boyfriend?"

"I don't know."

"What's his name? You do know his name, don't you? Or by boyfriend do you mean some one night stand you picked up on the street?"

"Joseph Biernacki."

He wrote that down.

"So you have no alibi and you hated Rita. That doesn't look very fucking good."

"You're going to need more than that."

"You used your credit card," he said, cryptically.

"What is that supposed to mean? What did I use it for?"

"You used your credit card when you called Quickie Courier."

"Quickie Courier? Why would I—oh shit." Things started to

make a little bit more sense. The other day a courier had been struggling up the stairs with a large box when I came in—"Are you telling me Rita Lindquist was in the box that arrived on Monday?"

"I don't need to tell you that. You already know that."

"Someone killed Rita and mailed her to the CPA in the office next to me?"

I'd walked by the box and that was where the courier was delivering it. Gardner just stared at me.

"When I came into my office on Sunday morning there was a note from Rita. She said she was going to make me sorry."

"Except she was already dead."

"Well, I actually have no idea when she was in my office," I said. Then I tried to remember when the last time I was in there, before Sunday morning, when was I—Saturday morning. Early? Or was that Friday?

Gardner was staring at me, his eyes watery and bloodshot. "You're going to tell me eventually, you know. But please, take your time. I'm on triple time in about thirty minutes."

"Let me get this straight," I said. "You think I killed Rita, put her in a box, and then mailed her to the office next to mine."

He sighed heavily as though this was all too silly. "No, you mailed the package to an address near the river. An address that doesn't exist. You used the CPA's office as your return address."

"That wasn't very smart of me."

"I thought I'd be polite and not point that out," Gardner said.

"Where did I mail the package from?"

"You brought it into the Quickie Courier location in Evanston. "

"Did I? You have a witness? Someone who saw me carrying the box into—"

"We were given your general description. I feel pretty good about you being picked out in a lineup."

So, did that tell me anything? Was Rita's murderer someone who looked roughly like me? I was tall and thin and had brown hair. I looked like a lot of people.

"My fingerprints aren't on the box."

"Yeah, the courier told us you were really careful not to touch it when he asked for your help on the stairs Monday. I assume you wiped down the box after you packaged up Rita."

"And then I carried it into a Quickie Courier office? Wearing gloves? Your witness said I was wearing gloves?"

"We haven't finished analyzing the prints we took off the box."

"See there's a problem here. If I sent the box to an address downtown, then I was hoping to get rid of it. But it came back, basically because, as you say, I'm an idiot. Now you're telling me I knew the box was returned on Monday and I didn't do anything about it. That makes me an even bigger idiot."

I watched Gardener. He didn't say anything.

"I know you don't like me, but do you really think I'm that dumb?"

He pretended to think about it for a moment and then said, "Yup."

"How was she killed?"

"Please stop asking questions you know the answers to. You were looking for her. We know that. The two of you were in a gunfight last week."

"She shot at me. That's not a gunfight."

"In Chicago it is."

I sighed and looked up at the ceiling. There was something I was trying to figure out, but he kept interrupting me. What was it? Something to do with my office—the last time I was there it was clean. Or rather it was the same. That's what it was like when I came out of the office and found the courier in the hallway, so my office was obviously not a murder scene. If she had been killed there, if someone had cleaned it up I would have noticed differences. Things would have been moved. There'd have been the smell of cleaners. There was no way she was killed in my office. She was killed somewhere else. So, where?

"Where was she killed?"

"We're looking closely at your office."

"I was in there Sunday morning. It looked the same.

Nothing was moved. There wasn't any smell of cleaners. I mean, even if she was strangled, well, you know people release their bowels. There's always some mess to clean up."

His eye twitched. I was making him angry. That meant I was at least a little bit right. He said, "Why don't you tell me more about cleaning up the mess."

"You mentioned Rita shooting me. That's my motive?"

"Yes."

"If we're going to court you're going to make a big deal out of that, right?"

"You bet your ass."

"When she shot me six months ago the bullet made a mess of my shoulder blade. I have trouble picking things up. You know, like corpses and shit."

That sparked a few more eye twitches. "Don't think for a moment that a fucking doctor's note will get you out of this."

"Oh, I'm sorry, I was under the impression that murdering someone and mailing them away might require picking the body up."

The eye twitching had spread to a clenching jaw.

"So what. You had help."

"Yeah, I put an ad in *The Reader*."

"You need to take this seriously. You're in a fucking lot of shit."

"I didn't kill Rita Lindquist. Sooner or later you're going to figure that out."

His eyes narrowed. "You're a cocky son of a bitch."

He was right, I was. I guess that happens when you don't have much to lose.

"So… how did I kill her? Did I shoot her? Strangle her? Poison her with arsenic?"

He lost his temper completely and blurted out, "What did you do with her fucking head and her fucking hands?"

I'm sure my mouth fell open. Then I said, "Hold on. Are you saying the body you have doesn't have a head or hands?"

"What did you do with them?"

My mind was scrambling, trying to find something to hold onto. Something that made sense. I asked, "Is it even Rita?"

"Of course, it's Rita. We found a driver's license belonging to a Regina Lawson taped to the bottom of your desk drawer." He said that as though it made sense. It didn't.

That just made my theory stronger. "It's not Rita Lindquist."

"We know she was living as Regina Lawson. And you have her license. Her forged license. If you didn't kill her why would you have that?"

"Why would I have it if I *did* kill her? Why would I keep it? It incriminates me, doesn't it?"

"Souvenir."

"Am I a serial killer now? Am I the Boston Strangler?"

"I don't know why the fuck you kept it, I just know you did. I also know that anyone who kills another human being isn't working off the same kind of logic as the rest of us. I'll know why you kept the license when you tell me why you kept it."

I leaned forward over the table and said, "Don't hold your breath."

Chapter Three

WE WENT BACK and forth like that for a couple of hours. Eventually, Gardner got bored and took a break. I got to sit in the room all alone for another hour. It was close to dinnertime and someone brought in the bologna sandwich I'd been promised. It was dry and disgusting, but I ate it anyway.

It wasn't Rita. That I was sure of. It couldn't be. I also figured out that she was trying to frame me for her death. I mean, it was obvious. And smart. She was on the run. People would stop looking for her if she was dead, right? And, of all the people looking for her, I'd kind of proven I was the one most likely to find her (probably because I was the only one actually devoting time to it). So, framing me for her death was an elegant solution to her problems.

If I was right, it did leave important questions with no answers. Who was the girl in the box? Who killed her? Was it Rita who killed the girl? Or did she have her minion do it? And why was Hamish Gardner going along with this? If I could figure it out so could he, right?

Gardner took another stab at getting me to confess after dinner, but I decided I'd said enough and started keeping my mouth shut. I was sure I'd managed to find out all I could from him. His blood pressure rose with each question. I mean, they were the same questions so I started saying, "I already answered that."

"Answer it again. "

"No, thank you."

I was thwarting a basic police technique. He wanted to see if he could catch me in inconsistencies, that was easy enough to figure out. But "I couldn't physically have done this" was pretty easy to stick to. It was true, after all.

Eventually, I was left alone for a few more hours. Well, maybe more than that. Finally, a uniform came in, cuffed me—in front this time, much more comfortable—and took me to the bathroom. He watched me pee. That was a delight. Then he led me downstairs and out the back of the station. It was night. Midnight? Maybe later. There was a paddy wagon parked there with its doors open. Inside, five men sat on two metal benches. They were young, old, black, white and brown. They were high on something. Every last one of them.

The uniform pushed me into a spot next to the nearest guy —tall and white with bad skin. Then he shackled my feet to the floor and slammed the doors shut.

Almost immediately, the smell of stale booze and vomit in a small space was overwhelming. That bologna sandwich nearly made a second appearance. In a few minutes we were off. We were on our way to Cook County Jail. I knew that from my days as a CPD officer. I'd loaded people into the back of a paddy wagon myself. Many times. Once or twice I had to clean up after a drunk or a hype.

That left me thinking back to my days on the job. Honestly, it was pretty shitty. Dirty. Thankless. So why had I been so upset when I got forced out? That was almost seven years before and I could barely remember the person I was then. He was very different from me. He was rigid and stubborn and angry, very angry, and I was… well, I was still some of those things. But my life *was* different now. Very different. For one thing, I was the one being shoved into the back of a paddy wagon.

I probably should have asked for my phone call, but who would I have called? I used to have a lawyer friend, but now I wanted nothing to do with him. Didn't trust him. I could have called a stranger, I suppose. A lawyer I didn't know personally. But that was awkward. I could just imagine myself saying, "Hi, you don't know me but I've been accused of murder so I thought I'd call."

The ride down to 26th and California took about a half hour. There wasn't a lot of traffic in the middle of the night. None of us spoke. I was sure we were all wondering how we got into this mess and how we'd get out—or maybe not. Maybe we were finding it hard to want. No, that wasn't true. They all wanted something, another drink, another fix. I was the only one who didn't want. I didn't want anything.

There were no windows, just a grate that opened onto the front cab so that the driver could hear if there were any problems. I lost all sense of where we were. He stopped at red lights. Took a few turns. Finally we came to a full stop. I heard the front door open and shut when the driver got out. Then we waited.

One guy, a black guy, started to moan like he might throw up. The guy next to him threatened to cut his balls off if he did. Showing incredible restraint, the first guy didn't puke. Abruptly, the doors opened and a guard stood there in an intimidating black uniform. A CPD officer stood behind him. The guard didn't tell us his name, he just started talking.

"When I call out your last name, I want you to answer with your first name. Rodriguez."

"Here."

"Here? Here Rodriguez? Did your mother have a sense of humor?"

"Sorry, Johnny."

"Sorry Johnny Rodriguez. That's still a funny name."

"Johnny."

"Thank you. Willis."

"Edgar."

The guard continued calling out names. I looked behind him trying to get my bearings. I'd been to Cook County Jail before. To visit. It was a big place tucked behind the main

Courthouse where I'd been a lot more often. I knew there had to be some logic behind the different buildings. This one for female prisoners, that one for male. One for the more dangerous criminals. But I had no idea which was which.

The guard called out everyone's name but mine. Then he told the others to get out of the wagon. The uniform stepped forward and closed the door on me. I was going somewhere else. Probably maximum security. I mean, it made sense. They did think I'd killed a woman and divided her into parts. That made me at least a little bit dangerous.

We drove for a few minutes and then stopped again. The uniform got out of the front and then I waited again. When the doors finally opened, I saw that the paddy wagon had been backed up to a loading dock. There were two guards standing there. One held a clipboard and the other the plastic bag I'd filled with my belongings back at Town Hall Station.

The uniform leaned in and unlocked the shackles at my feet and then undid the cuffs. Then he backed up.

"Come out of there," the guard with the clipboard said.

I climbed down out of the paddy wagon. As I did, I glanced at the name tags the guards were wearing, Winger and Tagget. Winger was holding the clipboard while Tagget held my pathetic plastic bag.

"Welcome to Cook County Jail," Winger said with a certain amount of sarcasm. "Whether you're here for a few days or a year, you'd be well advised to learn the rules, follow the rules, keep your head down and your mouth shut. Big surprise, we don't want to be here anymore than you do. The easier you make things for us the easier they'll be for you. Follow me."

They led me through a double set of doors, a guard in front of me and one behind me. Once inside we stopped at the first room to our right. It was a room about twenty feet by twenty feet, with metal shelves against one wall. The shelves were stacked with beige uniforms. There was a metal table in the center of the room. On it was a large clear plastic bag to go with the small one I'd already filled.

"Take your clothes off and put them in this bag," Winger said.

I kicked off my Reeboks, undid my 501s and let them drop to the floor. I stepped out of them. Then I pulled the rugby shirt I was wearing over my head. I folded the jeans and the shirt and put them in the bag.

"I can keep my gym shoes, right?"

"Yes."

"And my underwear and socks."

He didn't answer me. Instead he said, "Open your mouth."

I thought I just had. I opened it anyway.

"Lift your tongue."

While I was dropping my jeans he'd put on a pair of latex gloves. Now he dug his latexed fingers into my hair.

"Lift your arms."

He looked underneath when I lifted them.

"Drop your underwear and bend over."

I knew better than say no or to mention that I'd seen something just like this in a porno. I did as I was told. Winger popped a finger up my butt. No KY. Burned like hell. Then I got to stand up and pull my underwear back on.

"That would be a lot easier if you learned a little something about foreplay." That slipped out before I really thought about it.

Winger stopped and stared at me. "I think I said something about keeping your mouth shut." Then he pushed a short stack of beige uniform at me. It was really just a shirt and drawstring pants. They looked a lot like medical scrubs except the shirt said DOC on the back.

Tagget had been looking over my Reeboks, probably to make sure I hadn't gotten them at the James Bond store and wouldn't click my heels together to have razor sharp knives pop out of the toes.

He gave them back to me. I had the pants and shirt on. They were huge and I was swimming in them. I stepped into my sneakers. Not exactly hard since the laces were in my little plastic bag, which was now inside my big plastic bag along with my clothes. Tagget took my arm and with a black permanent marker wrote the number 1025 along the inside of my forearm. I guessed that was my new identity.

After that, they handed me a stack of things to carry—towel, sheets, a bar of soap, a toothbrush, a small tube of toothpaste—then led me back to the hallway and further into the building. We went through two sets of locked doors. The building was old and every surface was thick with layers of paint. The current color was curdled cream. The doors we passed and the bars we walked through were all chipped and I could see that everything had once been tomato red, mint green and even sky blue.

I wondered if they'd consulted a color specialist to determine which color was most soothing to prisoners. Or did they just go to the hardware store and buy up all the paint that had been mixed by mistake? The latter seemed more likely.

Once we got to the actual cells it was darker. Only a few of the lights were on. I was in cell 1025—imagine that—on the first floor in the back corner. The door to the cell was thick metal with only a small window for the guard to look through. Winger took out an ancient-looking key and opened the door.

On one side of the room was a metal bunk bed, on the other a toilet and sink in one unit. The light in the center of the ceiling was on. Someone in the top bunk snored. Winger gave me a little push into the cell and then shut the door behind me. I set the things I'd been carrying onto the lower bunk. I sat down next to them.

I tried to think about the last time I'd slept, really slept. Saturday. The night I was supposed to have killed Rita. I would have laughed if I had the energy. Instead, I leaned over onto the thin mattress, my head landing on the bare pillow. I was asleep in seconds, not even completely in the bed.

———

HE WAS ALL NOSE, not much chin and a receding hairline. His eyes were a bulging, brilliant blue and he had long, dark eyelashes. He was hanging upside down from the top bunk staring at me.

"Steven Head," he said, when he saw that my eyes were open. "Armed robbery."

"Nick Nowak. Falsely accused."

"Oh me too, me too. I mean, yeah, I robbed a liquor store, but I left the gun in the car. Honestly, I was a little nervous so I totally forgot the gun and had to pretend. And now they won't believe me 'cause they found the gun when they picked me up. The world is an unfair place, man."

He hopped down from the upper bunk and I saw he was a short wiry little guy in boxers and a wife-beater. He went over to the toilet and took a long noisy piss. I would have tried not to pay attention, but he kept talking while he did his business.

"You go for your bond hearing yet? Fifty thousand dollars, the judge said. 'Cause of the gun. The one I left in the car. I mean, how fair is that? Yeah, I only gotta come up with five grand, but if I had five grand I probably wouldn't have been robbing a liquor store, you know? There's kinda this connection. When you're broke, you gotta take some initiative."

He shook his dick and dunked it back into his boxers. When he turned around, he said, "So come on, give. What'd you do?"

"They say I killed a woman and chopped off her head and hands," I said, hoping that he'd believe I did it and shut up.

"But you didn't do it."

"No. I didn't."

"So, why do they think you did?"

"I'm being framed."

"Who's framing you?"

"The woman they think I killed."

He stared at me a minute and then he cracked up. "Oh come on, that's dumber than my saying I left the gun in the car."

"So you didn't leave the gun in the car?"

"No, I—" He blushed, realizing he'd admitted he'd had the gun all along.

I sat up and stared at him. "When's breakfast?"

"Twenty minutes or so. They'll come by and open the door. Then we go out to the common area. It's Thursday so there's sausage gravy. Make sure they put it on everything."

"Shouldn't you get dressed?"

"Probably," he said, then he climbed back up onto the top bunk. He wiggled around putting his uniform on and making the bed squeak. And, of course, he kept talking, "I called my mother and asked her for the five grand. She's got it. I knows she's got it. She said she'd pay five grand to keep me in jail. Which I didn't think was very motherly, you know. That might be part of my problem, though. Having a mother who's not motherly." Suddenly, his head was hanging over the edge again, "So what's it like cutting someone's head off?"

"I wouldn't know. But I'll go out on a limb and say it's messy."

"You gotta have a strong stomach. I think I'd puke in the middle of it. Did you? Did you throw up?"

"I didn't cut anyone's head off."

"Yeah," he said, doubtfully.

Our door opened and it was time for breakfast. Turned out Steve was right about the gravy. It did make everything better.

Chapter Four

I CAN'T.

Two very small, very depressing little words. The sum total of Joseph's good-bye note. Over the past few days, I'd repeated them in sadness and anger, empathy and confusion, and frustration. Always frustration.

No one could. I thought he'd understood that. No one ever could, until they did. We all woke up each morning, unprepared, unable, the world against us. And then we did; moment by moment, we did. And when the heart of someone we loved was on the line, there was never a question. We did. No matter what.

How could Joseph not see that?

Of course, I didn't have a lot of time to dwell on thoughts like that. Steve Head did not shut up all day. Thankfully, a guard came to the door around three, opened it, and said, "Nowak, come on out."

I did. He cuffed me. I noticed he was holding my big plastic bag. "Am I getting a new cell?" I wouldn't have minded. Listening to my cellmate was wearing thin.

"No. You're going to bond court. We bring your stuff in case you get lucky. But don't get too excited. You won't get lucky."

I wasn't excited. I knew that a murder charge often carried a sky-high bond, and I'd need a lot more than five grand to get my ass out of County. My only hope of getting out was a silver-tongued attorney, and since I hadn't even made a phone call it was very unlikely I was going to find one on the other end of this journey.

The guard led me through a tunnel that went to the courthouse. That was when I realized the part of the jail I was in was directly behind the famous courthouse. It was the oldest part, I was pretty sure of that, and Al Capone had once stayed there. At least I was in good company—or bad, depending on how you looked at it.

In the basement of the courthouse, we reached an elevator. When the doors opened he said, "Face the back, keep your mouth shut." We went up one floor.

"All right, turn around."

We stepped into an open area that offered three possibilities, all lockups. I was led to the one on the far right. I'm sure there was some sorting principle, but I had no idea what it was. Inside the lockup were about eight men of various ethnicities, all wearing street clothes.

The guard took the cuffs off me and opened the door. He put my plastic bag on a set of shelves next to the elevator.

"I'll be back for you in about forty-five minutes."

The lockups had bars on all sides. In the other two, prisoners were talking to their attorneys through the back bars. There was a wide hallway on that side of the lockups and a door that probably led to the court.

I sat down on a bench, closed my eyes, and let my head hang. I didn't want to think about what might happen next. They weren't going to give me a public defender, I had too much money in the bank for that. I was either going to have to represent myself or ask the judge to hold off until I could arrange a lawyer. If I did the latter, I was going to have to go back to my cell and repeat this whole process at a later date. Neither option was appealing.

Nearby, someone cleared his throat. I ignored it. Already I was getting used to the random noises that came with constant contact with other human beings.

He cleared his throat again.

Then the guy sitting next to me kicked my foot. I looked up at him.

"You have company," he said.

I glanced at the back of the lockup and there on the other side of the bars was my former-friend and sometimes lawyer Owen Lovejoy, Esquire. He was short and thinner than the last time I saw him. He wore gigantic glasses that made his pretty brown eyes look enormous, a thin mustache and freshly styled brown hair. He wore a three-piece charcoal gray suit and a pink tie with a blue stripe. I walked over.

"What the fuck are you doing here?"

"Darling, I could ask you the same thing. Now we don't have much time so let's skip the personal rancor and get down to business."

"No," I said firmly. "Why are you here? I didn't call you."

"Yes, I noticed that, and I'm trying not to take offense. Really though, it's one thing not to invite me to a party but not inviting me when you've been charged with murder, well that's just plain rude."

"I don't trust you."

"Good. I don't want you to trust me. I don't want you to trust anyone. Trusting people only leads to disappointment."

He waited for me to say something. I didn't.

"All right, fine, if you must know there's a group in the CPD trying to start a gay officers' group. I've done a little pro bono work for them. One of them heard about your predicament and called me. We really do have to hurry. This is just a bond hearing and it's going to be very short. Do they have any actual evidence against you?"

Now I had a new option. I could represent myself, ask for enough time to call a lawyer I liked or at least didn't know, or I could go with Owen. I sighed heavily. Shit.

"Someone got ahold of my credit card and used it to mail a body to a nonexistent address downtown. The return address was the office next to mine, so that's where the body ended up. When they searched my office they found a license belonging to

Regina Larson—one of the aliases Rita Lindquist has been known to use."

"So the corpse is Rita?"

"They think so, but I think they're wrong."

"Who do you think the dead woman is?"

"No clue. But it's not Rita."

"Where were you when the woman was killed?"

"Sleeping."

"Alone?"

"Yes."

"Darling, you pick *now* to sleep alone?"

"Believe it or not I didn't know I'd need an alibi." I leaned in closer. I didn't want anyone to hear this part, "I've got a little money from selling Harker's condo, but I won't be able to go above a half a million."

The state would keep ten percent of the bond, fifty thousand on a half-million. Fifty thousand that I'd never see again no matter what. Fifty thousand that I could also use to pay for my defense.

"We'll worry about that when we get in there," he said, which was very unlawyerly. Most of them wanted to know how they'd be getting paid before they'd even open a file. "Meanwhile, to convince the judge to keep the number low I'll have to sing your praises while denying everything about the ASA's case. Is there anything else you can tell me that will help me do my job?"

Unfortunately, I hadn't recently saved any children from drowning, so there wasn't anything I could add. I shook my head no. A bailiff came in from the court and began calling numbers, "158, 214, 377, 897, 1025."

I showed Owen my forearm and said, "That's me."

"See you in a bit," he said, scurrying off.

Once the lawyers were gone, the bailiff unlocked each of the lockups one at a time. Those whose numbers had been called stepped out into the area behind the lockups. I was last. We went through the door directly in front of us, putting us in a sort of gallery with a thick Plexiglas wall that was hazy and badly in need of a good cleaning. There were three rows of uncomfortable seating all bolted to the floor. Up near the ceiling were a couple of speakers so we could hear what was going on the courtroom.

The courtroom consisted of a row of seating much like the one we were sitting in, and two small tables very close together, one for the prosecution and one for the defense. An ASA sat at the table on the right with two filing boxes full of the day's cases. Today's ASA was a harried looking woman who appeared to be just out of law school. The frown lines on her forehead suggested she'd begun to regret her Juris Doctor.

The defense attorney, a young woman in a mannish suit, was talking as I sat down.

"Your honor, my client is the sole support of three small children. If he's not granted recognizance he could possibly lose his job."

The ASA spoke up, "The defendant is accused of breaking a stranger's jaw in a bar fight. It's reasonable to suppose he might come into contact with strangers again."

"The victim threatened my client. He was only protecting—"

"Enough," the judge said. He sat behind the only nice feature off the room, a polished mahogany bench that was raised up into the air and looked a bit like the bow of a boat. "Bond is set at twenty-five hundred dollars. Miss McNamara, suggest to your client that he enter a rehabilitation facility. I'm sure the state's attorney would look favorably on that."

The bailiff pulled a file from a large stack and called out, "Case 377."

The ASA remained at her table, flipping quickly through her folders to find the case. Meanwhile, a different attorney stepped up to the defense table and opened his briefcase.

Before anyone could speak the judge said, "I think I know this person. 377 please stand up. A few seats down from me a scrawny black guy stood."

"Yes, I remember you," the judge said. "Heroin, isn't it?"

"Your honor my client has a family—" his attorney began.

"Yes, I've let your client out on I-bond a couple of times. Bond is set at two hundred and fifty thousand dollars."

"What? Your honor—"

"No, no, no," Case 377 started saying.

"Bailiff, inform the jail hospital that Case 377 will be detoxing there this weekend."

"Yes, sir."

"No, no, no."

"Your honor this is—"

"Appeal the bond next week. If your client is sober and contrite we'll talk." He nodded to the bailiff, who pulled out another file and handed it to the judge. He called out, "Case number 1025."

As that was my case, I barely noticed a bailiff coming to lead the sobbing Case 377 off.

"Owen Lovejoy, Esquire, for the defense, your honor."

The judge took one look at Owen and very nearly rolled his eyes. That was not a good sign.

The ASA launched into it. "Your honor, the state asks for no bond in this case. Mr. Nowak killed and then decapitated a young woman making him not only a flight risk but a danger to society."

"Allegedly," Owen said. "Your honor, the state has no evidence connecting my client to this murder."

"He has no alibi," the ASA said.

"The murder took place in the middle of the night on a Saturday. Do you have an alibi?" he asked the ASA. "What about you, Judge, were you sleeping alone Saturday night? Maybe we should lock you up."

"All right you've made your point," the judge said, then asked the ASA, "Is that really all you have?"

"Of course not. The defendant used his credit card to messenger the body—"

"And not a single credit card has ever been stolen in Chicago?" Owen asked, snidely.

"And we have a witness at Quickie Courier who describes—"

"I'm sorry he's not actually a witness until he picks my client out of a lineup. The best you can say is that my client fits the description given. Not that there aren't literally hundreds of men in the city—"

"Yes, thank you, I understand," the judge interrupted.

"Your honor, we have a lineup scheduled for Monday afternoon."

"And my client will be there."

"The seriousness of this crime—"

"What's her name?" Owen asked.

"Who?"

"The victim."

"Rita Lindquist."

Owen knew the victim's name, of course, he just wanted to start tossing her name around. And he wanted the prosecution to kick that off. He went right for the heart of the matter. "Rita Lindquist is herself a wanted criminal with many, many enemies. If that is indeed who this woman is."

"What does that mean?" the judge asked.

The ASA answered, "Your honor, we believe Mr. Nowak removed Ms. Lindquist's head and hands to hinder our ability to identify her."

"Wait. Are you telling me you're not a hundred percent sure who the deceased is?"

"We're fairly certain your honor."

The judge looked shocked. "Fairly certain?"

"Her license was found hidden in the accused's office."

"A license that said Rita Lindquist?" Owen asked.

"Well, no…an alias she was known to use."

The judge was looking very confused. Owen took this opportunity to step in. "Your honor, Mr. Nowak is a lifelong Chicagoan who has deep ties to the community. He runs his own private investigation agency and has a right to take part in his own defense. I have to point out that over the years he has assisted the police in numerous—"

"—and also 'assisted' a notorious mobster, Jimmy English—"

"What's that?"

"The accused was employed by—"

"Your honor, previous employment is not something that should be considered. We're here about a murder—"

"Mr. Lovejoy, what's the name of your firm?"

I was sunk, of course. Cooke, Babcock and Lackerby were well known for representing Jimmy English and a number of other career criminals. The judge would be well aware of that. No matter the evidence, I was not going to escape the suggestion of guilt my defense brought to the table. That was a shame. I thought I had the judge on my side for a moment there.

"All right, all right, I've heard enough," the judge said. "Bond is set at one million dollars."

Owen said, "Thank you, your honor." Although for what I had no idea. I didn't have ten percent of a million: a hundred thousand dollars. Jesus Christ. That meant I was going to be stuck in Cook County Jail until I took a plea bargain or went to trial. And, if and when I went to trial I'd be paying an attorney *and* an investigator. Life was getting suckier by the minute.

The bailiff led me back to the lockup I'd been in before. I didn't see any guards on the other side so I sat down on the bench. I was going to have to make some decisions and probably fairly soon. Did I want to keep Owen Lovejoy, Esquire, as my attorney? No. I didn't. Did I want to find a new attorney? No. I didn't want to do that either. So, which no did I want to say yes to? Honestly, it was just easier to accept Owen's help. I didn't relish the idea of sitting at a payphone calling strangers and asking them to help me.

He was going to have to find me an investigator, someone who'd do what I told them. I had no idea who that might be. Owen might have some suggestions. Since he was here, I wondered if he'd try to arrange a meeting with me. Probably not a bad idea to get some of these things ironed out.

"1025."

I looked up and saw the guard standing there. Time to go back to my cell. He opened the lockup and let me out. Then he went over to the shelves and picked up my plastic bag. He handed it to me and said, "Sorry, you're gonna have to change here. I'm not walking you back over to your cell and then bringing you over here again."

"I don't understand. What's going on?"

"You got bond. It's time to get dressed and get the fuck out of here."

I quickly got out of the jail garb—to a couple of catcalls from the prisoners in the lockups—and put on my own clothes. I took my wallet, my keys and my money out of the smaller bag and shoved them into my pockets. Then the guard led me out a door, down a narrow hallway through another door, and into the lobby outside bond court.

Owen sat on a bench on the other side of the lobby. I walked over. "I don't understand."

"You made bond."

"You paid my bond?"

"No, dear, they don't let lawyers do that. Some kind of conflict of interest thingy."

"So how did it get paid?"

"I had a blank check. All I had to do was fill in the amount."

"Whose check was it?"

"I'm afraid I can't tell you."

I shook my head. "Attorney-client privilege. Are you having déjà vu? Because I certainly am."

Our falling out had to do with his keeping secrets from me on the Jimmy English case. He'd pretty much kept me in the dark the whole time. He claimed attorney-client privilege. I didn't like it. "You're fired."

"You can't fire me. I don't work for you."

"You just represented me in court."

"I work for the people who paid me."

"You can't represent me against my will."

"Are you really going to turn down a free lawyer? You're facing a murder charge. You do have some idea how expensive that can get, don't you?"

I did.

"Reach into your pocket and give me a dollar."

"So I can fire you?"

"No. Well, yes, but… if you pay me then we'll have privilege and I can't tell the other person who's paying me anything you and I discuss. What that means is I can only tell them what happens in court because it's public. I can only tell them about the case against you, that's public too. Other than that, I can only tell them things you direct me to tell them."

Standing there, I tried to think. Around us, people rushed here and there trying to repair tragedies or avenge them. I was doing neither. If anything, I was trying to prevent a tragedy. I mean, it would be a tragedy if I went to prison, right? Mentally I knew it would be, but I wasn't in a place to connect with it.

I was tempted to just go home and sit in my apartment until they came to take me away again. I wanted the world to go away or at least forget about me. I wanted to drink until I felt sick and then sleep until I felt better and start the whole process over again. Then I had a thought, one that just popped into my head like a pink grenade: Sugar Pilson France.

Sugar was the most likely person fronting my bond. I mean, my friend Brian had money too, but I didn't think he had that much lying around. No, Sugar was the only person I knew who could comfortably drop a hundred grand. And if it was Sugar then I didn't mind what Owen told her. He could tell her everything. I was fine with that. If it was Sugar, I had to at least try to get out of this mess.

I reached into the front pocket of my jeans and pulled out a five. I handed it to Owen.

"I said a dollar. But if you want to start out by overpaying me I won't stop you."

"I guess you're my attorney."

"Wonderful. I really need to run, darling. I have a car. Can I drop you?"

Normally, I might have stubbornly said no. He was my lawyer now but I was still pissed at him. However, a cab ride home from 26th and California would cost a fortune and public transportation to and from the courthouse was a disaster. A

huge blunder in a city so well planned. Either that or a deliberate punishment imposed on the city's impoverished criminal
element.

I walked out of the building with Owen expecting to walk a
couple of blocks to his car, but by car he'd meant limousine. It
was sitting at the bottom of the courthouse steps. When he saw
us the chauffeur jumped out and came around to open the back
door.

Owen climbed in. I slid in after him.

Chapter Five

"HAVE you ever had sex in a limousine?" Owen asked as soon as he'd raised the partition behind the chauffeur.

"As a matter of fact, I have," I said, truthfully.

"Yeah, me too." After a moment, he said, "I suppose you're still too angry to—"

"I'm not fucking you."

He sighed dramatically. "Pity. Angry sex is *so* fabulous." We rode in silence for a bit. Then he said, "If we're not going to have sex, we should probably talk about your case."

"Why?"

"Because I'm being paid." Of course, if we'd been having sex he'd have gotten paid for that too. So I didn't quite see the problem in billing his client several hundred dollars an hour to ride silently in a limo.

"I'm going to ask you something I *never* ever ask a client."

"Oh goodie," I said.

"Are you innocent?"

"Of course."

"Ugh, that makes this so much harder."

"Really? Why's that?"

"Guilty clients lie about everything, even things they don't need to lie about. And when they get caught in a lie they just tell a new one. But an innocent client doesn't lie about anything. So even one tiny little white lie will make you look guiltier than an actual guilty person telling lie after lie."

There was, unfortunately, some sense in that.

"You're going to say as little as possible," he instructed.

"Fine by me." Absolute silence would have been nice. I really wouldn't have minded.

"So…who do we think the dead woman is?"

I thought for a moment. "I imagine she was someone Rita was conning and decided she was done with."

He smirked as though he had a secret. "I've been a busy boy. I've already requested the preliminary autopsy from the medical examiner."

"Aren't you supposed to ask the ASA for that?"

"Technically. But they'll try to hold it until the toxicology report comes in. That will take weeks. The medical examiner is new. I'm hoping she's still fuzzy on protocol."

I doubted he'd have any luck with that.

"You know," he continued. "We may not even have to find out who this woman is. If we can simply prove she's not Rita Lindquist then you'd have no motive."

"I suppose you're right."

"Of course I'm right. Your motive is half their case. Any sane person would want to kill Rita Lindquist after what she did to you. Take that away and they have to explain why you'd kill a Jane Doe and deliver her to your own doorstep."

"Rita's the one who killed Jane Doe. You know that, right?"

"It crossed my mind. She's trying to frame you. Is that what you think?"

"So she can get a fresh start. If the police think she's dead they're not going to look for her."

"Yes, there's that. And she's got an accomplice, doesn't she?"

"Yeah, there's a lot of heavy work here."

"So, you think she's got a male helper?"

I nodded.

"One who wouldn't mind decapitating a woman and removing her hands. Would that be hard to find? I don't know much about straight men."

That was a bit on the facetious side. I frowned at him and said, "Yes, I think it would be hard to find."

"So he might be someone she already knew?"

"That's possible," I said. It was also kind of interesting. I needed to look at Rita's life before she went on the run. How much contact had she maintained with her past? Was there anyone she trusted enough to tell where she was hiding? Would she ask people from her past for help?

"I assume you'll be doing your own investigating. I could still hire someone," Owen said. "Most people accused of murder are at least a little bit traumatized."

"I *am* traumatized," I said.

For some reason he smiled as though I'd just lied. He didn't get it. I knew I looked like I was fine. I had a bad habit of not displaying my emotions. Not that I didn't have them. I was a wreck and I'd be a wreck until the charges were dropped. Well, that's not true. I was a wreck when the police burst into my apartment. I was going to be a wreck for a long time no matter what happened.

"Yes, I'll be doing my own investigating."

"Well, let's agree that you're not going to go off on your own. If I ask you to find something out you need to find that out—and just that."

"Fine."

"Priorities. Proving Jane Doe is not Rita. We need to find out if Rita had any distinctive marks, moles, tattoos, scars. Next: possible helpers. Who did Rita know before she went on the lam? Who has she known since?"

The car came to an unexpected stop. We were deep in The Loop on Jackson Boulevard. I recognized that we were in front of Owen's building.

"I can take the El from here," I said.

"Oh no, Tito will drive you home," he said, meaning the chauffeur. "It's on me."

I gave him a look.

"Well, it's on the client. But there's no reason you shouldn't benefit."

He sat there for a moment not getting out of the car. Finally he said, "This is where you say thank you."

"You wouldn't have come if you weren't being paid."

"I'd like to think that's not true."

Now it was my turn to be silent. After a moment, he frowned and said, "Fine. Whatever."

He lowered the screen to the front seat and said, "Tito, take the gentleman wherever he wants to go." And then he got out of the car.

I gave Tito my address.

———

TWENTY MINUTES LATER, I stood outside my apartment bracing myself to go in. It was going to be a mess. I was sure it had been searched thoroughly and nothing put back where it started. I knew this because I'd done it to enough people back when I was on the job. Something about being a policeman meant you believed everyone was guilty until proven innocent and probably not even then. The homes I'd searched had belonged to people who hadn't yet been convicted, but still I remember thinking the mess we left was exactly what they deserved. I was regretting that attitude.

I opened the door and walked into my living room. The sofa I'd been sitting on the day before was scattered around the room. The cushions had been ripped open, the zipper still closed, completely ignored. The fabric had been peeled off the arms. Luckily, the hospital bed we'd rented for Ross had been picked up days ago. Given the condition of the rest of my things, the CPD would have shredded it. Everything that had been on my shelves was now in a pile on the floor, as were the contents of my desk. I was sure my Baby Browning was gone. I didn't even look for it. Nor did I look for the Sig Sauer. What was the point?

The kitchen was a Pullman with tiny appliances and a limited amount of cupboard space. Yet, with everything that had been in the kitchen now on the floor, I had to give myself some credit for having made space for so much more than I'd thought I could.

My answering machine was on the floor. There were messages. I hit the button.

"Hi Nick, this is Brian. Um, you missed the meeting with Ross' doctors. It wasn't good. The KS is spreading, he has lesions on his liver and lungs. They can't give him any chemo because he's not strong enough. And there's so much scarring in his lungs that there's very little surface left to absorb oxygen. We talked about keeping him comfortable. It's not going to be long. Okay. Um, call me back. I hope it was okay to say all that on a message machine. I mean, I hope you're okay."

Another message began. "Nick, it's Brian. It's Wednesday. The police were just here. What's going on? They were asking us where we were on Saturday night. What happened on Saturday? I mean, you went home, right? What's going on? Are you okay? They asked for a list of all your friends. If you need something… call me."

And that was it. No other calls. I'd call Brian later. I had to finish this first. I went into the bedroom. My mattress stood against the wall with three long slashes across it. My clothes were everywhere. There was almost nothing left in the closet.

I purposely calmed my breathing. Somewhere in this mess there might be a green bag from Marshall Fields filled with almost twenty manila files. Rita's work product from when she was at Carney, Greenbaum and Turner. Of course, the police might have taken the files. Definitely they would have if they figured out what they were. I looked around for the bag but didn't see it. At first.

And then I began to see pieces of the bag scattered around in the mess. Then I found a folder on the floor underneath my pea coat. I pulled it out. It was labeled 618 Wells. That was familiar but I didn't know why.

Why hadn't they taken the file? I asked myself. I flipped through quickly and realized Rita's name wasn't anywhere in it. Technically, they wouldn't have had the right to take it. Well, if they knew I'd stolen the file from Rita's desk they could take it.

But they didn't know that. I saw another file and picked it up. It was about gossip columnist, Gloria Silver. I doubted this was related to any work Rita had done. Briefly, Gloria had been involved with the scam Rita and her boyfriend were running. This must be the file where Rita kept whatever she had on Gloria. I'd known it was there all along, I'd just never looked at it.

Searching the debris, I found three more files. All cases Rita had worked on. Honestly, I had no idea whether they'd be useful or not. But I had so little to go on it made sense to take them. After standing around for a while, I realized there was nothing else in the apartment that would be remotely useful. I walked out and locked the door behind me.

I walked down to Aldine then across to Clark. My office was half a block down. I expected it to be even worse than my apartment. It was. For one thing, the door was standing open. Immediately, I noticed they'd cut out a couple of one foot by one foot sections of the carpet. I'm sure they were testing them for blood, but that seemed stubbornly dumb. I mean, did they really think I'd chopped up some woman and then shampooed the shag carpet? I stepped into the lavatory. The sink was gone. I guess they assumed I'd washed blood down it so they decided to take it to the lab. I was beginning to feel like I wasn't going to get my deposit back.

Then there was my desk. They'd basically broken it into kindling. All the drawers of my file cabinet were open making the cabinet lean forward. In the midst of the debris, my answering machine was blinking. I pressed the button. The first message was Brian. "Hi Nick, I'll try you at home."

Then, "Nick, this is Jill Smith. It's Wednesday. The police were here asking about Rita Lindquist. Asking about you. They wanted to know if I thought you were violent. Did something happen? They wouldn't tell me anything. I thought you were coming in on Monday or Tuesday, but you didn't. Would you call me, please?"

The message ended and I noticed something on the floor that I was actually looking for: a blue notebook. The one Jill

Smith had given me. Inside were several lists of names. One was a list of dormant accounts that had suddenly been used. I'd researched them and found that most of the people were dead long before the access—meaning it was Rita who'd made the withdrawal.

One of the names was a man named Andrew Rapp. Rita had not only accessed his account but moved into his house when she learned he wasn't there. That meant I might be able to figure out from the notebook where she could have gone.

There was also a list of dormant accounts that hadn't yet been tapped. I'd gone through most of the list to learn which clients had passed away. I'd been planning to deliver the list to Jill the previous Monday, but my life had spectacularly gotten in the way.

I tucked the binder under my arm with the files I'd collected at my apartment, then I left. I didn't bother to close the door. I mean, what was the point, right? Most of what was in there was now garbage.

I walked back toward the lake and over to the Melrose. I needed peace and quiet to think about what I was doing. I should probably eat something, too. To be honest, I was feeling a little nauseated. Still, when the waitress came over I ordered a cheeseburger, fries and a Coke.

Then I began going through the folders. The first file I looked at was 618 North Wells. Inside were copies of an artist's rendering of a glimmering building and a floor plan for one of the floors. The rendering showed an attractive, sleek skyscraper that tapered as it rose but only a bit. There were a few notches taken out of the upper floors so that it began as a large rectangle at the base and the floors gradually became a cross by the top floor.

Behind the two drawings was a prospectus. NORTHWELL REAL ESTATE INCOME TRUST, LTD. It was a limited partnership allowing people to invest in the building. And that's when I realized—I'd read about this building. It was sitting half-finished down near the river. *But what did Rita have to do with it? Why had she made the file?*

I thumbed through the prospectus. It was about thirty pages. Most of what I looked at made no sense to me—I hadn't been lucky enough to go to an Ivy League school and take classes on how to be rich. I did find the names of the thirteen board members toward the end—presumably at least some of those people were the swindlers. There was an 800 number I could call should I have any questions about my investment.

I set that aside and picked up the file labeled Gloria Silver. I could have looked at this quite a while ago. But first I'd been shot and wasn't exactly thinking about the files and then, well, there was always something going on. Besides, Gloria wasn't really a problem. I mean, yeah, she saw me outside Jimmy English's funeral and said something shitty about Ross. Admittedly, he had been her husband's lover so I was kind of used to—

I'd opened the file and was staring at a single sheet of paper. It was a page from Gloria's medical file. It was not the first page. Her name was at the top of the sheet. It was a form and the doctor had filled it in by hand. It was a challenge to read. The important part was DIAGNOSIS. Next to that it said: The presence of herpes simplex, candidiasis, bacterial pneumonia and wasting compel a diagnosis of AIDS. Patient admits to possible exposure.

I stopped. Earl Silver, Ross' former lover, had given his wife AIDS. I couldn't breathe. I tried inhaling through my nose—it sometimes helped, just not this time. I slid to the edge of the booth, turned sideways, and put my head between my knees. I concentrated on breathing. Tried not to think about my racing heart or the waves of nausea that kept coming.

Jesus fuck. I didn't even like Gloria, but this wasn't about her. This was about all of it. Everyone we were losing, the good and the bad. And the way it didn't seem to bother—

"Honey, are you okay?"

I looked up and there was my waitress holding my drink. I sat up and took the Coke from her. I drank half of it in one gulp. The sugar would help settle me.

"Could you bring me another one of these?"

"Sure thing," she said. "Your burger will be ready in a minute. Do you still want it?"

"Yes, please."

She walked away. I kept breathing. It wasn't just that Gloria had AIDS, it was that Gloria had AIDS and I'd barely eaten all day. Lunch at Cook County Jail hadn't come with any gravy to hide its disgusting-ness. I drank the rest of the Coke. I couldn't read any more. I was done.

The waitress came back with my dinner and another pop. I stared at the burger for a bit, then I tried a french fry and it went down okay. I tried a few more. I took a bite out of my cheeseburger. It was amazing. I was starting to feel better. Then I ate everything in front of me like I'd never seen food before. I even ate the parsley. I ordered desert: apple pie a la mode.

The waitress brought the check and I took a twenty out of my pocket to cover it. I didn't need any change. It was just over five bucks, but I thought she deserved it since I'd kind of scared the crap out of her.

As I gathered up my binder and files, I realized something. Something pretty important. I had nowhere to go.

Chapter Six

I RANG the buzzer to Brian Peerson's condo hoping he wasn't home. Well, yes, I also hoped he was home—but if he was at home it meant that Ross was alone in his hospital room and I didn't want to think about that.

As I waited, I tried to calculate how long I'd known Brian. Four, four and a half years. Hard years. The kind of years that make your friends decide you're some kind of Calamity Jane and they start avoiding you. As though tragedy were contagious; as though it could be passed by a handshake or a kiss on the cheek.

The intercom popped on.

"Hello?" It was Brian. He was home.

"It's Nick."

"Thank God."

The door buzzed, a sound more appropriate to an electric chair than a door, and I walked in. The building was three stories, made of dark red brick and had a nicely landscaped courtyard. There were dozens of buildings just like it in Boystown. It also happened to be right around the corner from mine.

When I got to the third floor, Brian stood in the doorway. He was still a blond-haired, blue-eyed little twink, so pretty he nearly glowed. As I got closer I noticed the dark smudges under his eyes and the way the skin around them cracked when he tried to smile at me.

"How's Ross?" I asked.

"He had a pretty good day. His breathing sucks, but he was smiling. I was there until about an hour ago. Walter and his boyfriend came, so I decided to come home.

"Walter? Who's Walter?"

Brian giggled a little. "Nick, you don't know Miss Minerva's real name?"

"Um, no, I guess I didn't. Is she still with that short little white guy?" The last time I'd seen Miss Minerva Jones, she had a diminutive, middle-aged, white boyfriend who followed her around doing her bidding.

"There was a short white guy with her, but I don't think it was the same one. I think she trades them in regularly."

We were in the living room. I glanced at the very uncomfortable sofa I was planning to ask if I could sleep on. I didn't have what you'd call fond memories of it, but it was better than my shredded mattress.

"I'm out of vodka. Would you like a glass of white wine?"

"Sure."

Franklin Eggers, Brian's boyfriend, came out of the kitchen. He was tall and thin and I'd never really liked him. The smell of dinner wafted after him. "Hi Nick. I'm making pork chops, there's an extra one."

"I just ate, thanks."

Brian had poured me a glass of wine from the bottle on the dining room table. I set the files I was carrying down next to a brochure with 2100 N. LINCOLN on the front page in a bold font.

"So Nick, what is going on with the police?" Brian finally asked. "The guy who was here was pretty obnoxious and wouldn't tell us anything."

"Hamish Gardner?"

He shrugged.

"Likes to cuss?"

"Yeah, that was him."

"I was arrested for murder."

"What!? Oh my God, Nick!"

"Hold on. I need to get everything off the stove," Franklin said. "Don't say another word until I get back."

He flew through the kitchen door. I looked at Brian and shrugged, sipped my wine and then Franklin was back. We sat down and I told them everything that had happened. They interspersed the occasional, "You're kidding?" or "Holy shit."

"So who do you think bailed you out?" Brian asked.

"It was a million-dollar bond. They had to put up a hundred thousand. And they're not getting it back. I'm thinking Sugar."

"I talked to her this morning. I told her about the police coming by and she seemed surprised."

"I'll go down and see her. Maybe tomorrow or the next—"

"You can't. She's in Charlevoix."

Charlevoix? It took me a moment, then I remembered the last time I'd seen her there had a been a lot of luggage sitting around and they were getting ready to go to her summer place.

Of course, this raised the issue of how did Owen know where to find her? And how did she get the money to him—oh, that was easy. She had an accountant do it. But—

"So, who do you think the woman in the box is?" Franklin asked.

"Rita has a way of insinuating herself into people's lives."

"But killing someone just to frame you, that's so—"

"Yeah." I spun that around for a moment. It did seem extreme. Even for Rita. Not that even a simple murder isn't extreme.

"Opportunity," I said finally. "My guess is she had an opportunity to kill two birds with one stone. She got something out of it. For one, she's probably using this poor woman's identity."

"You know, I've never really understood, why she didn't just leave Chicago after they arrested her boyfriend," Brian wondered. "She could be on the other side of the world by now. Safe and sound."

"And broke," I said. "Her best chance to get more money is here. Not to mention she's found places to hide out."

"She's always lived here, hasn't she?" Franklin asked.

"Yeah, I think so."

To Brian he said, "Familiarity. I know it seems counter-intuitive, but she feels safer here than she would somewhere else."

Franklin was a hometown boy. So was I for that matter. Brian had come up from Springfield. Not a huge move but enough to make him believe moving was a good way to solve a problem. And maybe it was.

"But why not just hide and collect the money?" Brian asked.

"You mean, why kill someone?"

"Yeah. She didn't have to do that. She didn't have to try and frame you."

"Vengeance. Another reason not to leave. You can't get revenge if you're hundreds of miles away."

Franklin shivered. "I'd better go finish dinner."

After he left, I picked up the brochure for 2100 N. Lincoln and asked, "You thinking of moving?"

He shook his head and pointed to the kitchen. In a low voice his said, "Franklin got it for me."

"He thinks you should move?"

"He's trying to distract me. Get me to think about something besides Ross."

For a moment I caught a glimpse of how difficult Franklin's life must be just then. His boyfriend absorbed by his dying ex. He must feel terrible for Brian and jealous of Ross and terrible about feeling jealous.

"He's being amazing though," Brian said. "I don't know what I'd do without him."

It's annoying when people you don't like turn out to be pretty decent.

"I'm glad it's working out."

"It is…" he said, sounding a little surprised and happy all at once.

"The police destroyed my place. Do you think I could stay on your couch?"

"You can have the guest room."

"Guest room?" It *was* a guest room, but it had become

Terry's room. Terry was the seventeen-year-old we'd been semi-parenting. "Where's Terry?"

"Moved in with Scott." Scott was his thirty-two-year-old boyfriend who called him 'Champ.'

"Why didn't he tell me?"

"Because he knows you wouldn't approve."

"Do you approve?"

"I don't know, Nick. Life is short," he shrugged. "He says he's happy."

"This guy is probably going to dump Terry before he turns twenty-one," I pointed out. Typical behavior among guys who like them young. Chicken hawks.

"I know. But the relationship can still mean something to Terry. A couple of years is longer than Ross and I were together. I wouldn't give up that time just because it was short."

It was also longer than I'd been with Harker. Or Joseph. He was kind not to have mentioned that.

Franklin brought out two dinner plates and I sat with them while they ate. Franklin tried to keep the conversation away from anything challenging. "Did you hear, Madonna was in a porno? It was in the paper this morning. She's suing to keep it from coming out."

"I think I'll pass," I said.

"You don't want to see Madonna in an orgy?"

"Franklin, we're eating," Brian said. We were silent a moment, then he said, "Ross told me not to call his family until afterward. He said they can have his body, but he doesn't want to see them."

I flashed on my brief visit to their home in Normal to bring Ross home. They struck me as the type of Christians who were kind in the cruelest ways. "So there's no funeral?"

"He wants a party. That's why Miss Minerva was there. She's going to be the hostess with the mostest."

I really hated talking about this. I asked Franklin, "What else was in the paper this morning?"

"Enormous fire at Arlington Race Track."

"Arson?"

"I don't know. I think just old and badly designed. The papers call it a firestorm. Nobody got hurt. Not even the horses."

Okay, now that definitely sounded like arson. I decided not to say so though. Brian poured me another glass of wine. The conversation drifted. Brian mentioned a benefit he and Sugar wanted to do for Howard Brown. A costume party next Halloween. That seemed so far away. I wondered if I'd be in prison by then.

After they finished eating, we went into the living room and watched *Hill Street Blues*. It was a rerun. Franklin had seen it already and kept telling us what was going to happen right before it did.

———

THE NEXT MORNING I woke up not knowing where I was. It took a moment of focusing before I recognized Brian's guest room. It was a small room with too much furniture: a double bed, a desk where Terry had done his homework, a dresser. There was a Wham! poster on the wall. I sat up, my head fuzzy with last night's wine.

I didn't have any clothes with me, so I'd slept in my underpants and the T-shirt I'd been wearing since Wednesday. When I stood up, I immediately saw that Brian had put a short stack of clothing on the desk with a note:

Nick—

I'm at the hospital with Ross. I'm off work for a while. This should get you through today. If you don't want to go home, we could go shopping? Unless you're catching bad guys.

Brian

THE WAS AN IRONED and neatly folded white dress shirt, probably Franklin's since he was closer to my size, a clean pair of underpants and socks. I took a quick shower—well, not that quick, I had to spend a good five minutes scrubbing 1025 off my forearm—dressed, grabbed the blue folders and files, and walked down the street to the Melrose for breakfast.

I bought the newspaper, but after the waitress poured my coffee I decided not to read it. Instead, I walked to the back of the restaurant to the payphone that was situated between the restrooms.

I put a quarter in and dialed information. "Frank Connor," I said. "I think he's out in Edison Park."

"Hold for the number—"

"No, wait, wait, wait, I just want the address." I really hated that operators no longer actually spoke to you. Just pressed buttons that spit out recorded answers.

"7534 West Lunt."

"Thank you."

She hung up on me. I went back to the table, asked the waitress to borrow her pen, and wrote the address on a napkin. Frank Connors had been a detective with the CPD and worked with Bert Harker for many years. The last I'd heard was that he'd gone out on stress leave after things in the CPD began to change.

Since the seventies, the department had been under a consent decree to look more like the neighborhoods they policed, which meant the force had to hire more Hispanic and black officers, and fewer Irish and Polish. The change began at the street level and now, a decade later, was starting to affect detectives at the various precincts. This hadn't set well with a lot of the force, hence Frank Connors' stress leave.

Yeah, he was being a dick for not wanting to work with black officers, but I needed him. He'd been around long enough to remember Rita Lindquist's father. I figured he might be able to fill me in.

The waitress brought me an ABC omelet, hash browns and wheat toast. As I ate, I tried to remember what I already knew about Rita aside from the fact that she'd taken over her father's business. I knew that she'd been involved with a guy named Bill Appleton, who was now in jail awaiting trial for embezzlement.

I actually knew more about Appleton because I'd done a background check on him for Peterson-Palmer. He was a liar and scam artist from way back with a resume punctuated with an education he didn't receive and jobs he never held.

Rita had moved in on my job with Peterson-Palmer while I was otherwise engaged. She did the original background check. When they became suspicious of him, they asked me to redo her work. I learned that Rita and Bill had apparently fallen in love while she was investigating him. I assume she realized he was a con artist and that did it, she immediately fell head over heels.

After I ate, I walked around the neighborhood until I came upon my car. It felt like weeks since I'd seen the putrid-colored Lincoln. When I did find it, it was easy to pick out from a block away.

It started right up and I drove out to Edison Park. Edison Park, where the Harkers had also lived, was the neighborhood of Chicago where a lot of the CPD settled, especially the higher-ups. It was right at the edge of the city limits, where you could live in Chicago—required if you were on the job—and feel like you lived in the suburbs.

A little more than a half hour later I was cruising down Lunt. I pulled up in front of a long, low ranch house that was new sometime in the seventies. It was made of thin, yellow stone and sat on a nicely landscaped lot with a row of petunias running along the driveway.

I walked up to the front door and rang the bell. A woman answered. She was well put together, in her mid-fifties and wearing a trendy pink suit that had gigantic shoulders and flared at the hip. She had one big gold earring in her left ear and its mate in her hand. She was shoeless.

"Oh my God, if you're here to talk to me about some bizarre religion I just don't have time. I'm running late for a luncheon in Park Ridge."

"I won't keep you. I'm here to see Frank Connors."

"Frank?" She looked at me suspiciously for a moment. "Has he done something illegal?"

"No. I'm an old friend."

"Frank doesn't have friends."

"Bert Harker was my lover."

"Oh! I see." She finished putting her earring on. "Well, Frank doesn't live here anymore. We're getting divorced. I think. I don't know. He's gotten so bitter. Honestly, I think some of it is losing Bert, but I think most of it is...well, it's a different world than it was, isn't it?"

"Where does Frank live now?"

"He's got an apartment in Jefferson Park."

"Can I have the address?"

"Of course. He'd love nothing more than talking about the old days. For hours and hours," she said with a heavy dose of bitterness. She didn't give me the address though. I had to ask again.

"Oh my God, I'd lose my head if it wasn't screwed on. Sunnyside. He's on Sunnyside down in Jefferson Park. 5518 1A."

"Thanks."

It wasn't in Jefferson Park though. She was wrong. It was actually Portage Park. I had relatives there, and when I was a kid we went back and forth all the time. My mother loved the shops around Six Corners. There was a huge Polish community and some of the stores sold Polish delicacies. I remembered my parents dropping me off to play in Chopin Park with some cousins.

On Sunnyside, I pulled up to the address I'd been given. It was a brick courtyard building like Brian's, but also unlike Brian's. It was small, almost a miniature version of Brian's place. It made me wonder if, when they were building Brian's building on Aldine, they took the leftover brick and made a miniature of it out here on the northwest side.

I went to the first entrance on the right. After I buzzed, the door made that spine-tingling electric sound and I stepped into a closet-sized lobby. It was so small you had to shut the front door before you opened the door leading to the stairs. Apartment 1A was just up four steps on the right. Frank Connor stepped out of the apartment and stared at me.

"What are you doing here? I was expecting a pizza."

"Sorry to disappoint," I said, not mentioning that it was just past breakfast time. Most pizza places weren't even open.

He went back into the apartment, leaving his door open as he did. Inside, there were four small rooms: a living room and bedroom in the front, a dining room and kitchen in the back. There was a bathroom as you came in the front door.

The whole place was eerily empty. There was one towel in the bathroom; nothing in the dining room to my left; nothing in the bedroom in front of me, also on my left. The living room, where Frank had gone, was the only room with any furniture to speak of: two dining room chairs and a mattress. The mattress had a pile of bedding clumped together in the middle. One of the chairs held a portable TV tuned to the new Spanish station. Frank turned the TV down and sat in the other chair.

There was no place for me to sit, so I didn't. On the windowsill sat a pack of cigarettes and an ashtray. Frank was in the process of lighting a cigarette.

"You're not doing so well, are you Frank?"

"I'm doing fine."

"No you're not. You should apologize to your wife and go home. Try smiling once in a while."

He gave me a withering look that reminded me I wasn't in the position to give that kind of advice. I'd done such a good job of fucking up my own life I'd lost the right to tell anyone what to do with theirs.

"Is that why you're here?" he asked. "To tell me to smile?"

"No. I got arrested for killing a woman named Rita Lindquist." I assumed there were additional charges related to chopping up the body but I didn't bother to mention them.

Frank smiled. That didn't feel very nice.

"Did you ever run across her? Or maybe her father? They were P.I.s."

"I remember Gunner Lindquist. We all knew who he was. He was always around. Back in the old days, he was one of those peepers who used to try and get pictures of cheating spouses, things like that."

I waited. There had to be more than that. Frank took a long drag off his cigarette. I was tempted to ask for one—I mean, why not, right? But he started talking again.

"There were always rumors about blackmail. First it was about his switching sides in a divorce case. The wife hires him, then the husband offers to double his fee if he'll switch sides. That sort of thing. Then, later, there were rumors about his daughter—she must have been twelve, thirteen at the time. He'd have her meet men in a motel room. He'd get some photos and then blackmail the men."

"That can't be true."

"I said it was a rumor, so I don't know. Not for a fact."

I pushed away the thought of what that might have been like for a teenage girl and asked, "What happened to Gunner?"

"Dead. Two, three years now."

I nodded and said, "Lung cancer."

Frank made a face. "Um, no. Who told you that?"

I shrugged. "I don't remember."

"He showed up in the Chicago River with a bullet in the back of his head. That's not exactly lung cancer."

"It was a hit?"

"There's a building near the river."

Before he could continue I inserted, "618 North Wells."

"Yeah, that's it. Lindquist was involved in that somehow."

"You don't know how?"

Frank shook his head. "Financial Crimes has had an open investigation on that building for years. As near as I could tell they were conning people at every stage of development. They sold shares, too many shares, then they paid fake construction companies. The real companies, they cheated the employees and welched on their workman's comp contributions. They were even running a scam with stamps. They'd buy a hundred thousand dollars in postage stamps and then sell most of them to a dealer at a discount. Postage is not a suspicious line item. The amounts they were spending on the other hand…"

"I'm not seeing how Lindquist is involved."

"We were pretty sure he knew about at least some of the scams and was blackmailing someone over them."

"You don't know who though?"

"Could be any one of the people involved. It could be all of them."

"What about Carney, Greenbaum and Turner?"

"They were the attorneys for the finance guys *and* the construction companies. But given privilege we could never prove what they knew and when they knew it."

There are a couple of dicey rules lawyers have to navigate when dealing with the guilty. First, if they know of ongoing or upcoming crimes they should report them, and second, they can't help their clients lie about the crimes they've already committed. Many lawyers ignore those rules completely.

"Rita worked for them," I explained. "Did her father have that job before her?"

"Yes, I think so."

"So she might have something on them, whatever her father had?"

"And you think that's what got her killed?"

"I don't think she's dead. The body is missing its head and hands."

Letting that sink in, he crushed out his cigarette butt in a plastic ashtray. "You know, Bert and I worked a case. Seventy-eight, seventy-nine. This guy, we found him in the trunk of an abandoned car near Erie Park. He didn't have hands or a head. No I.D. They didn't want him identified, see. But the guy did have a tattoo. A mermaid. We went to fifteen, twenty tattoo places. This was when they still had a lot of tattoo parlors down on State Street, so maybe it was before seventy-eight. Might have been seventy-two. I don't remember."

"That's great Frank, but I don't have all day—"

"No, you have to listen. There's a point. The mermaid. We were able to make a preliminary identification based on the tattoo alone. One of the places we went into, the artist remembered it."

"No kidding."

"So you see…there's always a way."

"What about the car?" I asked.

"What about it?"

"Was it his car?"

"Actually, it was. But that wasn't how we figured it out. We followed the tattoo."

"Why wasn't the car registration enough?"

"The guy was a hired killer. We knew it might be him, but we also knew it might not be. See, that was the problem."

"Okay, Frank. I think I need to go now."

"Yeah, you know there was this other time—"

I held up a hand to stop him. "Look, go home to your wife and apologize. You're being kind of a dick. So just stop, okay?"

The empty look on his face suggested that he might actually listen to me.

Then I walked out. Frank's marital problems weren't my business. But given my own situation the idea of anyone getting over it, getting back together, well, I couldn't leave it alone. And besides, other people's problems are always less complicated than our own.

Chapter Seven

DRIVING AWAY, I wondered if I'd actually learned anything remotely valuable. I already knew the point of cutting off someone's head and hands was to hinder identification. The CPD thought the body was Rita. It wasn't. That was exactly as she'd intended. Nothing new there.

The thing with that building on Wells, that was weird. Rita's father was somehow involved. That involvement might have gotten him killed. If it did, there was one thing I knew for certain. Rita would want revenge. Was that why she had a file on the building? Was she planning revenge? The prospectus for 618 North Wells included the names of thirteen board members. I wondered for a moment if they were all still alive.

I drove back to Boystown and parked near the Belmont El station. I took the Jackson Park down to the city. It was time to deliver Jill Smith's overdue list.

Peterson-Palmer was located in a boring gray metal building on Adams between Clark and LaSalle. Jill Smith's office was on the fourteenth floor. She made me wait twenty minutes, which I shouldn't complain about since I'd promised her the list at the beginning of the week.

I spent the time reading an article on the front page of the *Daily Herald* about a plot to sell arms to the Iranians that the FBI managed to foil. Some lieutenant colonel was deep in it and likely would go to prison. I was reading about the various agencies involved in catching this guy when Smith's assistant told me I could go in.

Jill Smith was the kind of attractive, blue-suited woman you now frequently saw in the Loop. Yeah, they were still outnumbered by men ten-to-one, but a decade ago you rarely saw a woman who wasn't a secretary.

"I'm not happy with you," she said. "You were supposed to bring me that list of dormant accounts at the beginning of the week."

"Sorry, I had some things come up."

"You should have called me, I could have sent a messenger. I mean, we know Rita's out there attempting to access these accounts. This could have cost us a lot of money."

Apparently, she wasn't a newspaper reader. I stood there uncomfortably not explaining things. She picked up her phone and dialed four numbers. They had an internal intercom system.

"Could you come down?" she asked, well more commanded. Then she hung up. "Give me the list."

I opened the blue notebook and took out the list. Gave it to her. She quickly glanced at the names.

"These people are all dead?"

"Yes."

"I'm going to have the accounts frozen."

"No, don't," I said.

"Why not?"

"Because Rita might try to access one of them."

"But that's what I want to avoid."

"If she accesses an account that would help us find her."

"The police should be doing that, not us. Our responsibility is to protect the firm from financial liability."

"I've been accused of killing Rita," I admitted.

"Well, if she's dead then she can't access anything." I was a little annoyed that's where her mind went. She didn't seem at all concerned about how much trouble I was in or whether or not I might have killed someone.

"She's not dead. The body the police found wasn't Rita."

She looked at me a long moment. Then after a nod, she said, "I'm going to assume you didn't kill anyone."

"Thank you for that. I think Rita killed some poor woman and is trying to put the blame on me. It was all in the papers."

"It was in the papers that Rita's trying to frame you?"

"No. I mean, what's in the papers was wrong."

"Exactly why I don't read them."

Just then Raymond Dewkes, who worked in their MIS department, walked into the office. He was young, small and kind of sexy, despite the fact that he wore a white shirt with an ink stain flowering at the base of his breast pocket. He saw me and smiled—it wasn't until then that I remembered him flirting with me.

"Thank you for coming down, Raymond," Jill said, then looked at me, making her decision. "I don't think we need you after all."

"Yes, we do," I said, then immediately asked my question, "How long since you ran the report on dormant accounts?"

"About ten days."

"Can you run it again?"

"What? Why?" Jill asked.

"It's possible Rita may have accessed an account or two in the last ten days."

"Oh, right. I suppose that's true. All right, Raymond, rerun the report every morning until further notice. Does that work, Mr. Nowak?"

"Yes."

"What are you looking for?" Raymond asked.

"If Rita is able to access an account we may be able to find her."

"So you need to know which office she's gone into?"

"Yes, if you can tell us that, as well, it would be great."

"You realize there are other ways to access accounts," Jill pointed out. "Depending on the type of account: checks, wire transfers."

"But she'd need to have the checks or access to private information," I pointed out.

"Typically, mother's maiden name."

"She's going to stick to what she knows. She knows how to fake identities. Either she's taught herself how to forge a driver's license or she knows someone who's good at it."

Jill considered that a moment and then said, "As soon as you have what you need we should close these accounts," Jill said. "They represent a significant liability to the company."

"Of course. Should I wait for the report?" I asked.

"No, we run those reports at night," Raymond said. "They take up a lot of server space, so we try not to run them during the day."

"Okay, thanks."

"Do you really think she'll try it again?" Jill asked. "I mean, you found her at Andrew Happ's. She has to know we're looking at these accounts."

That was something to consider. Rita was nothing if not smart. "I don't know," I said. "She might not have a choice. Regardless, it would be foolish not to keep an eye on the accounts, wouldn't it?"

"Yes, of course. Sorry, it's just that our department gets charged for each report."

"Let's do it for a week. If we don't have her by then we'll think of something else."

"That's reasonable," Jill said. To Raymond she said, "So you'll have the first report for us Monday morning?"

"Sure thing."

———

TWENTY MINUTES later I was at Cooke, Babcock and Lackerby sitting across from Owen Lovejoy, Esquire. The offices at Jackson and Michigan Avenue were only a few blocks from Peterson-Palmer, so it didn't make sense not to stop by and see him. After all, he was, grudgingly, my attorney.

Wearing a pair of obviously new gold-rimmed glasses, he sat behind a large slab of glass sitting on a metal frame. There were a couple of filing cabinets and several boxes of files on the floor on one side of the room. Behind the desk, in front of a window that had a sliver view of Grant Park and the Art Institute, was a black credenza which held his phone and a large box-like machine that hadn't been there last time I was. I had no idea what it was.

"Congratulations darling, you're on page three of the *Daily Herald* and the front page of the *Tribune's* Metro section."

My stomach churned like a cement mixer. *Why didn't I know this?* I'd read the *Daily Herald* in Jill Smith's lobby but only the front page. Why hadn't I looked—

He recited from memory: "'Private Investigator Nick Nowak, 37, has been arrested for murdering fellow Private Investigator Rita Lindquist, 32, in an apparent turf war.'" He pulled a face, "Really, where do they come up with this stuff? Neither of you makes enough money for a turf war. They make you sound like gangsters."

"Do they mention the body in the box?"

"No, that'll be tomorrow's headline. 'PI puts woman in box, sends to self.'"

"Great. Today I'm a murderer. Tomorrow I'm a stupid murderer." I flashed on the possibility I was going to have to endure a long trial in which the state's attorney trotted out every dumb thing I'd ever done in my life to prove that yes, I was stupid enough to mail myself a corpse.

Owen was saying something, "What? I'm sorry—"

"I said, 'What have you done so far?'"

"Oh, um… I talked to someone I know on the job. He told me about Gunner Lindquist. Rita's father."

"I don't know that I can do much with that," Owen said.

"Someone killed him and left him in the Chicago River."

"Interesting. But it's not getting you off a murder charge."

"There's a building at 618 North Wells—well, half a building. It has a long saga of criminal—"

"Yes, I've heard the story. Tell me how it's useful."

"Well, I don't know yet. All I know is that Rita had a file on the building, so she was interested."

"How did you get a hold of that file?"

"Last winter I stopped by her office and picked it up."

He stared at me a moment, clearly aware that I was talking about a crime. "Well, let's not dwell on that, shall we?"

"All right."

"Don't spend much time on the building angle. It doesn't sound like it will lead to anything useful."

I wasn't as sure of that. I planned to follow it up unless I came across a more compelling lead.

"What else have you done?" he asked.

"I stopped by Peterson-Palmer. They're going to run a daily report to see if Rita tries to access any of their dormant accounts. We know she's already done that."

"So she'll be too smart to try it again."

"I'm hoping she's too desperate not to."

"Does she have another source of funds?" he asked.

"I don't know what it is, but I'm sure she does. Possibly she's draining the girl in the box's accounts right now."

"I got the autopsy about an hour ago."

"Did you?"

"I coaxed the medical examiner into sending it over Zapmail." He nodded at the machine I hadn't recognized.

"What's Zapmail?" I asked.

"Federal Express. Facsimile machine." That didn't make much sense to me. He went on, "Anyway, we caught a break right off the top. She refers to the victim as Jane Doe."

"Really?"

"The Medical Examiner isn't convinced this is Rita Lindquist. The report notes they've drawn blood and sent it for typing. And they're doing a search for Rita's medical records."

"They'll need to search her aliases too. She may have used one to go to the doctor."

"Do you know her aliases?"

I had to think that through. "Rochelle LaRue. Lingstrom. Randi, I think. Ruby no last name. And Regina Lawson, of course. Those are the ones I know. I'm sure there are more. What else does the autopsy say?"

Owen moved the report in front of him. It had that shiny,

degraded Xerox paper they used to use when copiers first came out. The kind I usually only saw in fiche machines these days. There were about ten curling sheets stapled together.

"It starts with the typical narrative. How the body arrived at the morgue. Still in the box. She talks about lifting the corpse out. Notes that there is no head and no hands. 'Victim was a well-nourished woman between the ages of twenty-one and thirty.'" Owen read forward a bit. "This is odd, she notes that the victim's toes are painted. That it appears she'd had a recent pedicure. And that it looked expensive. Why would she write something like that?"

"If we knew who Jane Doe was we could trace her final movements," I said, stating the obvious.

"Yes, but we don't know who she is."

"True, but it could still be useful. "An expensive pedicure suggests she was well off. Presumably she had a manicure at the same time."

Thinking about her hands made me wonder if there might have been defensive wounds. It was a shame we couldn't determine that. It's possible to have defensive wounds on your feet—if she were killed somewhere while she was naked, or at least barefoot, she'd have scrapes on her feet from struggling.

"Does it note any cuts, scrapes, bruising?" I asked. "Anywhere?"

"No. Oh, wait…" He read for a moment. "Whoever cut her head and hands off was a real amateur. The incisions on the neck and hands show hesitation marks. And, uh—bruising on 'posterior of the neck below the incision. Each bruise measures five to six inches.'"

"Does that suggest she was strangled with two hands?" I asked.

"It does to me. You have two hands, though, so it doesn't help us much."

"To be clear, she was strangled and then her head was cut off."

"And presumably her hands at the same time."

"Why do that?" I wondered.

"Well, so she can't be identified."

"No, that's not what I mean. If you're planning to kill someone why not poison them? Or simply drug them? Once they're out you can amputate to your heart's content. And Rita has poisoned before."

"Are you saying you think this wasn't planned?"

"Up to strangling the girl, no. After that, that does show planning. Or at least improvising."

"Your credit card was used. I assume it was stolen?"

"I think just the number. It's mostly for business so I keep the bills at my office."

"When do think Rita stole the number?"

"On Sunday morning I found a note on my desk from her. It said, 'You will pay for what you've done. I will make you sorry.'"

"Do you have the note?"

I had no idea if it was floating around with the rest of the trash on my office floor. "I don't know," I said. "And I don't know that it matters. It was typed. Probably on my typewriter. They'll say I did it myself."

"All right. We know that Rita was in your office the night Jane Doe was killed. Keep that in mind in case we can figure out a way to prove it."

"Did Jane Doe have any tattoos, scars, strange moles?"

"Nothing that's mentioned. Do you know if Rita does?"

I thought for a moment. "No, I don't. What about hair?"

"I don't see anything about hair."

"I think Rita's hair is red or reddish-brown. I mean, I think it's dyed black now. Or maybe blond, who knows? But she's originally a redhead. What about freckles? Are they mentioned?"

"No."

"Don't most redheads have freckles?"

Owen got a sly look on his face. "Well, the field research I've done would suggest they do. And then there's the pubic hair. Which isn't even mentioned here."

"Really?"

"It just says there were no signs of sexual trauma and that the genitalia appear normal."

"Rita's also very busty."

Owen smirked and then full out giggled. "Looks like I'm going to have an interesting afternoon talking about women's breasts and pubic hair with the ASA."

I stood up, ready to go. "I'm glad you enjoy your work."

Chapter Eight

I WALKED out of Owen's building not quite sure what I wanted to do next. It was after lunchtime, but I'd had my breakfast late so I didn't need to eat. I would have gone over to the French Bakery anyway, but I knew Brian wasn't there. And neither was Ross. I still knew a few people there but not well. There was something terrible about that. I hated that things changed. It always felt like a dirty trick.

For shits and giggles, I went down to the main library to look up a few people. Thirteen to be exact. I wanted to know more about the board members listed at the end of the prospectus for 618 North Wells. It was probably a dead end. A waste of time I didn't have. But I went anyway.

At the library, the first thing I did was look up everything I could on the building itself. I found short articles announcing that it was going to be built and describing it as a 55-story condominium with premium amenities. There would be retail space on the first two floors, another two floors of common area for the condo, including office space for a management company, a pool, a meeting room, a bike room and storage lockers. After that, for the next fifty floors the units themselves would range from studios to three bedrooms.

The only thing unusual to me at all about those first articles were that they went back to 1981. It seemed like a long time, but then maybe that wasn't unusual for a 55-story building. It wasn't really my area.

I also found articles about the limited partnership itself (later in 1981), the fact that the zoning board had approved the building design (1982), and one article touting the fact that the architect had won an award for his design (1983). Several names came up over and over: Richard Crisp, Anthony Papalopolus and Arturo Luna. They appeared to be the main movers and shakers behind the building, which would also make them the primary con artists.

I looked them all up. I didn't find much beyond their involvement with 618 North Wells. Except for Arturo Luna. I found an article detailing his suspicious death at the end of 1984. He'd been shot in the back of the head in his Highland Park garage. I also found an article on Gunner Lindquist, 56, of Niles, also shot in the back of the head right before he was dumped in the Chicago River early in 1983. Maybe there was a connection there.

Lindquist died first, then Luna. There was more than a year and a half between their deaths. Was it possible that Rita had something to do with Luna's death? That would certainly have been revenge served cold. It was also possible, though, that Luna was killed by whoever killed Rita's father—since the deaths were similar. If so, was there anything about Luna's death that would have led Rita to her father's killer? And if she knew her father's killer, had she taken revenge yet? Or was she still planning it?

After I printed out those articles, I went down to the wooden phone booths on the first floor of the library. I had nine quarters. My plan was to call as many of the thirteen board members as I could. Using the telephone book that hung on a chain under the black payphone, I looked up the name that had come up most often in connection with the building: Richard Crisp.

There were five Richard Crisps. Two were on the south side in neighborhoods it was very unlikely the Richard Crisp I was looking for lived in. That left three. I called the first number and got an answering machine. Something about the message made me feel like it wasn't the right guy. I hung up.

Then I called the next number. A woman answered.

"Hi, I'm trying to reach the Richard Crisp who's on the board of directors for—"

She began laughing. "Richie on a board of directors? This is a joke right?"

I agreed that it must be and said goodbye.

When I called the final number, a man answered. That was encouraging, except he didn't speak English. I said "Goodbye," and hung up.

That was three quarters down with no results. Crisp could easily have an unlisted phone number. In fact, it was very likely he did. If I had my name on a famously corrupt building in the middle of Chicago I'd get an unlisted number.

Giving up, I walked out to Michigan Avenue. It was warm, almost muggy. Clouds hung over the lake like a touchy-feely uncle. Close, I think that's what they used to call it. The air was close.

I let my mind go blank for a moment. I wasn't sure what to do next. A big part of me really wanted to grab a cab back to Brian's, get into bed, and simply pull the covers over my head. Then I got an idea.

I walked down to Randolph and crossed the street. It was one way going west. I turned around and stepped out into the street to wave down a cab. I snagged a Checker. It was one of the last, old and rattling. I loved it.

"Daily Herald Building," I told the driver. He plunged the vehicle back into traffic.

The Daily Herald was along the river, a low-slung, six-story building nestled among a quickly multiplying group of high-rise apartments. It was smudge-gray and I remembered from a high school tour that the actual printing press was on the first floor. The cab let me out at the front door. I walked in and went to the reception desk. Behind it sat a heavy-set black man in a navy uniform.

"Hi. I need to see Gloria Silver. Do you know if she's in?"

"I can call upstairs and find out. Who should I tell her is here?"

I knew damn well she'd never let Nick Nowak into the building, so I said, "Gunner Lindquist."

After he told Gloria who was calling, he listened a moment then said, "Tall, skinny, white guy. Needs a good shave." He watched me as Gloria had more to say. "Okay. Okay. Fine."

After he hung up the phone he took a deep breath. "That lady does not like you."

That wasn't good. I kind of needed to talk—

"But she said to send you up. Fourth floor."

As I walked toward the elevator he said, "And good luck."

"Thanks," I said. Hey, I'll take my luck where I can get it.

In the elevator, I was alone. Some big conglomerate had purchased the paper in the last year or so and I had the feeling its staff was now a lot smaller. I pressed four and then stared at the fake veneer on the elevator walls. The building was probably thirty years old and had not been built with pricey materials. It was starting to show some age.

That theme continued when the door opened and I was on the fourth floor. The space in front of me was an open hodge-podge of mismatched desks from the fifties and sixties. Some of them had CRTs on them, a few still had typewriters, many were bare. I stepped into the room and looked around. There were a couple of writers around, busily working, none of them were Gloria. To my right were some offices with glass walls. I craned my neck to see if I could find her.

"I'm over here," said a voice behind me. I turned around and Gloria was standing in the doorway of another glass office on the opposite side of the room. She was tall and slender; wearing a navy jacket, pleated white skirt, nautically-themed shell (semaphores) and a showy pair of navy-and-white Spectators. I had the feeling she'd bought the shoes first and worked her way up. Her hair was very blond, and blown out and moussed so it made her head look twice as big.

"Hello Gloria," I said.

She looked me up and down like I was a stain on her favorite blouse and walked back into her office. I followed her. Her desk was French provincial, either something she'd bought herself or something she'd demanded. Behind her was an antique credenza which held dozens of framed photos of her with local and national celebrities. Above that, in an elaborate gilt frame, a rather realistic portrait of her deceased husband, Earl Silver. It was a good enough likeness that I almost said hello.

"You know I was tempted not to let you up here," she said. "Am I going to regret this?"

I closed the door and sat down in her very comfortable guest chair. "I've been arrested for murdering Rita Lindquist. I'm out on bail. I'm surprised you haven't heard. It was on page three."

"Good God, you don't think I actually read the dreck we print? If it's not in the *New York Times* I know nothing about it."

Somehow I doubted that. Taking the file I'd been carrying out from under my arm, I said, "There are a few names I'd like to ask you about."

"You realize I don't know everyone in Chicago. Though I'm sure it seems like I do."

"Richard Crisp."

She left a short pause. "Richard is on the board at the opera. He's a well-respected businessman. Very charming. Well, very rich, and that's considered charming."

"Anthony Papalopolus."

"He owns that Greek restaurant in Old Town. Zorba's. I made the mistake of mentioning it once in the column. Now he calls every week hoping I'll mention it again."

"Elliot and Diane Buckman."

"The Buckmans are personal friends. What does this have to do with your killing Rita Lindquist?"

"I didn't kill Rita. In fact, I don't even think she's dead."

"Well, that's not very nice of you. Teasing me with the idea the bitch might be dead." Her voice was a combination of venom and sugar. "How could they arrest you for the murder of someone still alive?"

"They found a corpse in a box outside my office. No hands, no head."

She visibly shivered and stared at me for a long moment. From her desk, she picked up a glass paperweight. There were several more nearby. I guessed she must collect them.

"As interesting as that is, I don't see what it has to do with 618 North Wells."

"I didn't mention 618 North Wells."

"Yes, I know. I thought I'd save some time. The people you asked about are all on the board. I'm guessing you want information on the rest of the board?"

"I do."

"How tiresome."

"Arturo Luna."

She paused again. I thought she might throw one of the paperweights at me. That didn't stop me from saying, "I'm beginning to understand your relationship with Rita."

"What does that mean?"

"I talked to an old friend this morning. He used to be on the job. He told me that Gunner Lindquist had a long history of blackmailing people. I have a feeling the apple didn't fall far from the tree."

"You think Rita has been blackmailing me? Is that what you're saying?"

"No. I'm saying I *know* Rita has been blackmailing you."

"And how do you know that?"

"I have Rita's files."

Her face went pale and she looked out the window. It was a nice view down the river to the lake. I doubted it was comforting.

"Are you here to blackmail me too?"

"No. I would like you to tell me everything though."

"And how is that *not* blackmail?"

I didn't say anything. She sighed deeply and at first I didn't think she'd tell me a thing, but then she began. "I met Gunner

Lindquist through the Buckmans. It was before Earl died. I wanted to know... well, you know what I wanted to know. About your friend. Shortly after I took over the column, the paper hired an editor from *People*. She wanted some real dirt in the columns. Earl had always been too classy for that. I'd been trying to follow his lead but... I started using Gunner professionally."

"You told me you take 'tips' not to put certain things in the newspaper. Did Earl do that?"

"You have to understand. When I began writing *The Silver Spoon* the paper offered me half what they'd paid Earl. Which was terribly cruel because, if anything, it costs me far more to do the column. My clothing budget alone—even with the freebies I get—well, it's enormous. And people who used to tell Earl things for nothing wanted me to pay them. I was struggling. And—well, if I'm writing about someone, I have to call and ask if they'd like to comment. Most of the time they offer before I have a chance to ask."

"And then Gunner died."

"Yes. I read about it in the paper the morning after his body was found. The Buckmans were terrified. It was obviously a professional hit. They knew it had something to do with 618 North Wells. They really did think the building was legit at the start. By the time they figured out everything that was going on they were in too deep to walk away. Rita showed up in my office about six weeks after her father's death. Told me she was taking over his business. Told me my taking over for Earl had inspired her. Which, looking back, was probably bullshit."

"Rita likes bullshit."

"Well. I needed an investigator. The information Gunner found for me was very useful. I'd come to rely on it. So I gave her a try. Honestly, she wasn't as good as her father. I thought I could do better if I looked around, so I tried to fire her. That's when she showed me what you found in her files."

"I'm sorry," I said.

"And I'm sorry. I assume we're in the same boat. Fellow passengers, as it were."

We weren't; I didn't have the virus. I just smiled though. She could assume what she wanted. I didn't want to take the chance that she'd stop talking to me.

"Where was I? Oh, yes. Things got worse after that. She 'suggested' I become more involved in My Old Friend. The charity. They work with the elderly. Rita and Bill wanted names. Leads as they called them. Bill would sell them on an account at Peterson-Palmer and then they'd begin to slowly steal from them. I felt terrible about it."

"Not so terrible you didn't take your cut."

"I couldn't turn down the money. Rita would never have trusted me after that. And I have two girls. I'd like them to have a little something when I leave this world."

"And when the whole thing fell apart, you told the Feds about Rita's blackmailing you."

"Of course."

"And that's why they didn't prosecute you."

"That and the fact that I told them everything I could think of about Rita and Bill. I was very cooperative."

I nodded. Then I put her file on the desk for her. She opened it and looked at the top sheet.

"It's yours."

Quietly, she closed the file and slipped it into a desk drawer.

"Thank you."

"The woman in the box. She's close enough to Rita's height and weight that the police believe it's her. I suspect she has some connection to Rita. I'm not flattering myself with the idea that Rita deliberately killed someone to frame me."

"She saw an opportunity and decided to take it," Gloria said, having firsthand knowledge of that. "You think this young woman has a connection to someone on the board for 618 North Wells."

"It's possible. I assume someone on the board had Gunner Lindquist killed, as well as Arturo Luna."

"Richard Crisp," Gloria said simply.

"Rita has a taste for revenge."

"You're looking for a missing girl in her late twenties?"

"Yes."

"I'll make a few calls."

————

I HATED walking around with a beeper attached to my belt—I never stopped jumping every time it beeped. It did make life easier though. I gave the number to Gloria so that she could reach me if she found out anything important.

When I left the building, I thought about walking toward Michigan Avenue. I could catch the 146 Express there. It would meander along until right after the Hancock Tower, when it would merge onto Lake Shore Drive and get off at Belmont; a block below my apartment.

I could also stay on the bus all the way to Irving Park and then walk over to Thorek Hospital. I needed to see Ross. I hadn't seen him in days, but, honestly, I was afraid to. I knew he was getting worse. From the things Brian was saying I shouldn't waste any time. And yet when I thought about going my stomach felt like a stone.

My beeper went off. My first thought was that Gloria had already come through for me, but it wasn't the number at the *Daily Herald*. It was the exchange for Peterson-Palmer, but I didn't recognize the whole number. I was still standing in front of the Daily Herald on Wabash. I saw a sign for Don Roth's River Plaza, which apparently was at the bottom of a tall apartment building. I headed toward it.

I found the restaurant one story down from the plaza, next to the building behind a sunken courtyard. When I opened the door, there was a crowd of people in a cramped lobby area. Two frantic hosts were talking to each other attempting to get everyone seated. Even though it was early, the dinner rush had started. Written on a chalkboard were the specials and the phrase, HAPPY HOUR 4-7, which explained why they were so busy so early.

My stomach grumbled and I was tempted to put my name down. I went up to the hostess stand and before I could say anything a pretty young girl said, "There's at least a half an hour wait." The stress in her eyes told me she hoped I'd go away.

"I just need a pay phone," I said, deciding against dinner.

She breathed an obvious sigh of relief and said, "It's just beyond the restrooms. Go straight across the dining room to the back of the restaurant. If you look up you'll see a sign with an arrow pointing right."

"Thank you."

I walked through the dining room. It was busy, chaotic, a busboy and a well-dressed man—probably a manager—were clearing a table at lightning speed. I found the pay phone where the hostess said it would be, threw in a quarter, and dialed the number on my beeper.

"You beeped me?" I said when the phone got answered.

"Nick? This is Raymond Dewkes at Peterson-Palmer."

"Yes?"

"I moved a few things around, so I have that report for you."

"Okay. Is there anything on it?" It didn't make sense to go down there again if it there wasn't any information.

"There is. There was a withdrawal made on Wednesday. The thirty-first."

I waited. "Do you want to give me the details?"

"Well, I mean, I thought you could come back in. I get a dinner break in an hour and I know a place."

Oh. He was hitting on me. I thought about going back to Peterson-Palmer for a moment. I mean, why not? I was single now. There was no reason not to. And it might lighten my mood. But then another question occurred to me: Why? And I didn't have an answer for that. If I had, I might have gone.

"Uh, you know, maybe another time. Can you give me the information?"

"Yes. Of course." I could tell that I'd disappointed him. Oh well. "Uh, the withdrawal was made in our River North office. The name on—

"I thought all your branches were in the suburbs?"

"This one opened in March."

"Oh, okay."

"The account is Winslow Porter. Do you want his address?"

"Sure."

"He's at, or he was at, 300 North State, unit 3535."

It was nearby. I thought about where I was and then asked, "Is that Marina City?"

"Um, maybe. I don't know."

"Do you know who handled the transaction?"

"D. Blanski."

"And where is this office?"

"Hubbard and LaSalle. Um, 428 Hubbard."

"All right, thanks."

I was about to hang up when he asked, "I didn't offend you, did I?"

"No. I'm not offended. Just… it's not the right time."

"Well, you know, if there ever is a right time."

"I'll let you know."

I hung up and walked back up to street level. Coincidentally, both the apartment that Rita might be staying in and the Peterson-Palmer office where a check had been cashed were within a few blocks of me. So, what to do first? It was possible Rita was hiding out at the Marina City apartment. Bold, but possible.

That it was nearly five o'clock made my decision. I hurried over to the Peterson-Palmer branch to see what I could find out. I half-ran the four blocks down Hubbard and found the Peterson-Palmer office at the bottom of an older, ten-story brick building. My guess was it wasn't long for this world.

Walking through the glass door, I found myself in a lobby very similar to a bank's. I walked over to the nearest desk and asked a young woman in a smart, gray suit where I could find D. Blanski. She pointed at a desk across the lobby where an older woman sat. Even from across the room I could tell she was tightly wound. She also looked very professional and I suspected she set the tone in the office.

I went over and without being asked sat down in one of the leather guest chairs in front of her desk.

Looking up, she studied me a moment then glanced at her watch. She frowned. "Can I help you?"

"You're D. Blanski?" It said so on a little black at the front of her desk but it was worth asking anyway.

"I am. And you are?"

"I'm a private investigator working for Jill Smith in your main office. You handled a transaction on Wednesday for a Winslow Porter?"

She thought for a moment. "Oh, you mean the guy who got mugged. That was very sad."

"He? A man withdrew the money?"

"Yes. Winslow Porter is a man."

Of course it was a man. *What was I thinking? Was I thinking?*

"Was there a woman with him?"

"No, he was alone."

"And he'd been mugged. He told you that?"

"Well, no. He didn't. He told me a story about losing his wallet on a trip to the Indiana Dunes last weekend. But... well, he had scratches on his face and someone had given him a black eye, so I assumed he was lying. You know, the male ego."

Several ideas raced through my mind. First, the girl had fought back. She'd fought back hard. *Well, good for her.* And, Rita *did* have an accomplice. As much as I'd suspected it, knowing for sure left me uncomfortable. It was fairly obvious why he'd told D. Blanski he'd lost his wallet. He didn't have a picture ID. Did that mean something? Had Rita lost her forger? Or were things just moving too quickly?

"He didn't have a license and you let him withdraw money?" I asked.

"He had a temporary paper license. We don't normally accept those but given the circumstances. Plus, he knew his social security number. By heart."

"A paper license would be easy to forge," I said.

She flushed from the neck up. "Are you saying he wasn't Mr. Porter?"

"How old was he?"

"Late twenties, early thirties."

"You didn't check his date of birth, did you?" It would have come up on her CRT with the other account information.

"What, er, no. I guess not." Nervously, she asked, "Porter's an old man, isn't he?"

I nodded. "How much did you give him?"

"Five thousand, I think. I'd have to check to be sure."

"What did he look like, aside from being young and having a big bruise on his face?"

"He was tall."

"Taller than me?"

"Could you stand up?" I did. She calculated. "Yes. A little bit."

"Six four," I guessed. "What else?"

"He had sandy hair, blue eyes, not much of a chin."

I was a little offended. He had to be the same guy who'd used my identity to mail the dead girl. I had a chin. Not to mention, my hair was brown and my eyes were hazel. He looked nothing like me.

"Did he flirt with you?" I asked.

"Of course not. I'm a professional."

"I didn't ask if you flirted with him. I asked if he flirted with you."

She thought. "He might have. I try not to notice. It's not a good idea to get offended. And it's an even worse idea to be flattered."

"Any distinguishing marks? Tattoos, scars, moles, birthmarks."

"Beady."

"What?"

"His eyes. He had beady eyes. Like a rodent."

This just got worse and worse. My eyes were not beady. I asked, "How was he dressed?"

"A little shabby. You might think that should have been a tip-off, but a lot of our clients dress like that. The ones who still have the first penny they ever earned."

I took a moment trying to think of anything else that might help me.

"Am I going to lose my job?" There was real fear in her face so the next part wasn't much of a surprise. "I'm divorced. I've got two teenagers. My ex stopped sending support checks years ago."

She looked around. I had a feeling this wasn't information she shared at work.

"I wouldn't know about your job either way," I said. "It's not up to me to decide."

"Of course not. It's never really up to anyone and yet these things get decided, don't they?"

Chapter Nine

I FOUND myself standing across the street from Marina City trying to figure out how I'd get into the building. I'd already checked out the garage. There were a couple of valets standing around. It seemed like they were always there. Apparently, if you lived there you never had to park your own car—which sounded like heaven.

Even though I hadn't found the front entrance I was sure there'd be a doorman. Even if I walked in confidently and tried to breeze past him—as I often did in office buildings—there would be locked doors to deal with.

Wait. Rita had been living at Andrew Happ's Lincoln Park home just the week before. Yes, I'd left her without a place to live, but would she have been able to insinuate herself at Marina City so easily? Was this the best choice on the list of dormant accounts? And who exactly was the tall guy who'd made the withdrawal from Winslow Porter's account?

There were a few things I knew for sure. Rita had had the list of dormant accounts for more than six months. Andrew Happ died in early May and Rita passed herself off as his niece about a month later. How did she know it was safe to move into his house? And where had she been before that? If I could figure out her pattern, I might know what she was doing.

If she was researching the list as I had, she'd have figured out which accounts were worth investigating further. Just like me, she'd have searched for obituaries. Those were people with families who were deconstructing a person's life. They hadn't found the dormant account, but they would have sold their relative's home or moved in themselves. Yes, there was still time to access the account, but she needed information and a fake ID. That took time and she couldn't risk the family finding the account before she got to it.

No, she'd have focused on the dormant accounts owned by people who were isolated somehow. They could be senile or so estranged from their family that the family didn't even know they'd died. Or, like Andrew Happ, they could be a John Doe in the morgue.

So, what had she been doing? Had she created 'safe houses' for herself all over Chicago? And was there one on the thirty-fifth floor in the tower looming over me?

I found the residential lobby back toward the office building next door. It was a bland room with a big, circular desk and a couple of square brown leather chairs. There was a locked metal door leading to the elevators on the other side of the room.

Behind the desk was a youngish white guy with a half-dead stare. I went up to him and said, "My name's Nick Nowak. I'm a private detective. I'd like to ask you a few questions about a tenant."

I got my card out of my wallet; one of the small stack onto which I'd carefully written my beeper number on the flip side.

The doorman had a name tag that said, "Wally." He placed my business card onto the desk in front of him as though I'd just given him something of great value.

"Unit 3535, Winslow Porter," I said. "Do you know who I'm talking about?"

"There's like 450 units."

"That's a lot of people."

Wally laughed.

"But you know some of the people who live here?"

"They know me. They say hi I say hi back."

"Can you call Mr. Porter for me and see if he's at home?"

"Oh, um, okay." He opened a plastic notebook. Inside were pages upon pages of phone numbers belonging to the 450 units. Wally flipped through. The names were alphabetical. I watched as he flipped all the way through and began looking through the W's."

"P," I said. "Porter. His name last is Porter."

"Oh, okay."

He flipped back and missed the P's a couple of times. I was about to recite the alphabet for him when he stumbled upon the P's; possibly by accident. Starting at the beginning, he ran a finger down the columns. Finally, he found the phone number and dialed. He listened for about thirty seconds and then hung up.

"Mr. Porter is in Paris."

"For how long?" I asked.

"Um, he didn't say."

"You got an answering machine, right?"

"Yeah."

"Can you call again so I can listen to the message?"

He thought about it for a long moment and then said, "Okay." He dialed again and then handed me the phone.

"Hello. This is Winslow Porter," he said. The way he pronounced his name was very grand. "I'll be in Paris until early nineteen eighty-six. If you're a friend of mine you've already got my number in France. If you're not a friend of mine don't bother to leave a message. I won't call you back."

I handed the phone back to Wally. It wasn't a good idea to leave a message like that. It was like asking to be burglarized. Apparently, Mr. Porter had confidence in the building's security. After just a few minutes with Wally, I didn't have any.

"There are other entrances to the building, aren't there?"

"Uh-huh."

"What are they?"

"There's a commercial plaza downstairs. Residents have an entrance to that."

"And a loading dock?" I guessed.

Wally pointed at something in front of him. I stood on my

tippy-toes and looked over the desk. Under a shelf were five TV screens hooked up to security cameras positioned all over the building. One watched the loading dock, another what looked like the entrance to the commercial plaza, two were trained on fire exits, and one watched the valets park cars.

"So, you watch TV all day?" I asked.

"Yeah."

"Must get boring."

He leaned forward. "I used to work the night shift. Two of the valets had a hooker come by and give them BJs. I called the police. Got them fired." He seemed very proud of that, and more attentive than I would have thought.

I nodded. The loading dock was probably the best way into the building, but it was a two-person job: one to distract Wally, while another entered through the loading dock. Not something I could do on my own.

"So you're on days now, Wally?"

"Kind of. Three to eleven. Monday through Friday."

That suggested there were two other shifts during the week. They probably had two guys take care of the weekends with twelve-hour shifts. So, five, maybe six security guards. I suspected Rita had made her way past one of them.

"Thanks, Wally. You have a nice day," I said, and walked out of the building. Winslow Porter's apartment was going to have to wait. I needed to find out more before I worried about how to break into unit 3535.

Though I already had an idea how to do it.

––––––

THE CAB DROPPED me off in front of 2137 North Hudson. Andrew Happ's house. It was Victorian with a gray stone façade, two-stories with a raised basement and ornate wooden stairs leading up to the first floor. It was topped with some green metal work. The house looked placid, as if to deny that there had been gunfire in front of it just the week before.

I walked over to the house just to the south of Happ's. It

also had stairs up to the first floor. This house was red brick though. I knocked on the front door. After just a moment, a small, attractive woman with her hair pulled back into a thick ponytail opened the door a crack. I could smell dinner cooking behind her, or rather dessert, something with chocolate. We'd met before, the sour look on her face attested to that.

"Do we have to do this? Do you know how many times I've talked to the police in the last week? Six. The last time was yesterday. All the questions were about you. They say you killed Ruby—I mean, Rita. Whatever."

I decided not to ask to come inside. "They haven't even proved that Rita's dead."

"They sounded pretty sure."

"They found a box with a woman's body. No hands, no head."

"Jesus Christ."

My beeper went off. I ignored it, saying, "They think it's Rita. I disagree."

"What do you want with me?"

"Just a few questions. Rita was here for around two months?"

"Yeah, I guess."

"Was she here the whole time or did she go away for a few days on and off?"

"I don't know, maybe. I don't pay that kind of attention to my neighbors."

"Was she always alone?"

"She had friends. Everyone has friends."

"Tall guy? Sandy hair, blue eyes, chinless."

"Yes," she said, uncomfortable that I knew that. "He was here a lot. I asked Ruby if he was her boyfriend, but she said 'no.' She only kept him around because there were people after her."

"So he was violent?"

"No. I mean, I never saw anything. From what she said I thought he was, you know, protective."

"And a young woman, roughly Rita's weight and height?"

She had the decency to go pale. "I saw a woman like that one night. The three of them got out of a cab."

"Did you hear them use any names?"

She shook her head.

"Did you notice anything about this girl? Anything at all."

"It was late. Dark. They were dressed like they'd been out dancing."

"So they might have picked the girl up?"

"I didn't think so at the time, but yes, I suppose." She was obviously uncomfortable with three single people having a three-way.

"When was this?"

"It was really hot. I couldn't sleep, otherwise I wouldn't have seen them at all. It must have been July. Maybe the beginning of July?"

"And you only saw the girl once?"

"Just that one time, yes."

"Did you notice her hair color?"

"Light brown, maybe blonde. Dirty blonde. Like she'd used too much Sun In. I didn't really get a good look." It sounded like she'd gotten a *very* good look.

"Can you think of anything else that might prove useful?"

"I don't—Ruby was kind, she was friendly, she was a good person. I don't know if I believe any of this."

"Bad people don't announce themselves. Don't beat yourself up because you can't see it."

"I, I can't talk about this anymore. I'm sorry."

She closed the door in my face. I took the beeper off my belt and looked at it. I recognized my lawyer's phone number. He was working late on a Friday night, I suppose that was good. I had barely enough time to get to the hospital and see Ross. Visiting hours ended at eight. Feeling like a heel, I decided to go back to Brian's and call my lawyer.

After my second cab ride of the day, I walked into Brian's condo. It felt silent and lonely. I could tell I was there alone. I went into the kitchen and opened the refrigerator. Franklin had cooked the extra pork chop the night before and left it in plastic wrap. I unwrapped it and ate most of it over the sink. When I was done I threw away the bone and went out to the living room where Brian kept the sleek, white cordless phone he'd just bought. I dialed my lawyer.

It was after hours so he answered his phone himself.

"This is Nick," I said.

"Tell me you've found Rita."

"Not yet. I did find out she has friends. A very tall man and a woman about her age. Andrew Happ's neighbor saw the three of them together in July."

"What was color was this girl's pubic hair?" he asked.

"I have no idea. The hair on her head was light maybe blonde, maybe dyed."

"Dishwater?"

"Possibly."

"The pubic hair on the corpse was light brown. The carpet should match the drapes. Did you ask about this woman's breast size?"

"Sorry, I forgot."

"That's fine. The corpse was about a B-cup according to the medical examiner. You described Rita as busty. That's at least a C, possibly more."

"When did you learn so much about bras?"

"An hour ago. From Padma Kirkland, the pathologist who did the autopsy. We're buds now."

"She sounds fascinating," I said, not that interested. "There was a withdrawal made on one of the dormant accounts. Client named Winslow Porter."

"Really? I was sure she wouldn't dare."

"She didn't. Her tall friend is the one who made the withdrawal."

"When?"

"Two days ago."

He sighed heavily. "That doesn't really prove anything."

"It proves she has an accomplice."

"Who might have killed her. I could at least throw suspicion on him."

"She's not dead."

"I believe you, dear. But I also have to think about what I can get a jury to believe. Is that all you have?"

I thought about mentioning Gloria Silver, but her health didn't seem relevant and he'd already said he didn't want to know any more about 618 North Wells.

"No, that's all I have."

"Well, I have some news. And it's not good. I called the ASA to discuss pubic hair and women's breasts. He was not impressed."

"That's to be expected."

"And… they have a witness. Steven Head."

"I don't know who that is."

"Your cell mate at County. He says you confessed to him."

"You're fucking kidding me."

"Oh, I wish I were."

"The guy talked so much I could barely get a word in. I couldn't have confessed to him even if I wanted to."

"Apparently, you told him details that only the killer would know."

"Didn't happen."

"Well, I didn't think so. Someone's out to get you, dear. Any idea who?"

Chapter Ten

BELIEVE IT OR NOT, things got worse from there. The ASA was planning to go back to the judge and ask—given this "compelling" new evidence—that my bond be revoked. That meant I had until sometime Monday to figure this whole mess out.

The last thing I asked Owen before I hung up was, "Who's the ASA you're dealing with?"

"Tony Stork."

I knew Tony. Intimately. I also knew he was married, which meant he was susceptible to blackmail. And Rita Lindquist was Miss Blackmail 1985.

"FYI, Tony sucked me off in an interview room, probably three years ago. During the Campbell Wayne prosecution."

"I doubt you'd be believed," Owen said. "It looks desperate."

"I am desperate."

"Sometime you'll have to tell me all about it, though. Blow by blow."

I didn't appreciate the fact that he could make jokes. I wasn't feeling all that funny. I said goodbye and tried to figure out what to do next. I had to find out who the tall guy and the dishwater blonde were. They could be connected to the list of dormant accounts. They could be connected to 618 North Wells. They could also be people Rita picked up in a bar. Or through the personals. Or a hundred other ways con artists meet their marks.

Making another trip to the kitchen, I found a half-full bottle of white wine in the side-by-side refrigerator and poured some into a coffee mug. I was too lazy to bother with a wine glass.

Think like Rita, that's what I had to do. I'd taken away her playmate in December. She would have been on the lookout for a new one shortly after that. She'd want someone she could trust. Someone she felt safe with. Possibly someone she already knew. I wondered if Bill Appleton had any ideas. Or his ex-wife.

Brian kept a pad next to his phone. I grabbed it and wrote down those two names. Who else? I could try to find someone at Carney, Greenbaum and Turner who knew her. Like my attorney, they'd probably be working at least a few hours on Saturday.

Gloria Silver. Hopefully, she'd call me with some information. If she didn't call by Sunday morning, I'd give her a nudge. I could go back to Andrew Happ's neighborhood in the morning. On a Saturday, there would be more neighbors to talk to. There might be more to find out there. Maybe.

I sipped my wine wondering where Brian and Franklin were. Visiting hours were over so they should… Then I remembered it was Friday night. They might have gone out to dinner, maybe a movie. The kind of things normal people did. I also remembered that Friday was the night Joseph went to a group for ex-priests and nuns called Open Church. That's where he met Alejandro. It made sense they'd be there tonight.

I didn't know where the group met, but it couldn't be that hard to find out. I could go there and—and what? Yell, scream, shake him, beg him. I could tell him I'd been arrested for murder, make him feel guilty he wasn't with me, helping me, supporting me.

What good would any of that do? It wouldn't bring us back together. It wouldn't change any of the reasons he'd left me. A line had been drawn, a line that was being drawn everywhere for gay men. Joseph was on one side with Alejandro and I was on the other. As much as I wanted to be on his side of the line, as much as I wanted to be with him, I couldn't be. This was something I couldn't fix and I felt helpless.

Brian and Franklin came in about nine with Chinese takeout and a big brown grocery bag. Nobody asked how my day had gone—it was that easy to figure out it hadn't gone well. Franklin took the Chinese into the kitchen. As he dug through the grocery bag, Brian said, "They moved Ross to the ICU and put him on a ventilator."

"Shit."

From the bag he produced a bottle of Absolut, one of tonic, and a small bag of limes. He got three tall glasses out of the built-in sideboard. Franklin came back in with a tray of ice. Brian made three drinks without asking if I wanted one. It was all too obvious that I did.

A ventilator. We were close to the end. It wouldn't be making him better, it would simply be extending his life. Shit.

"We've been lucky," Franklin said.

"You're fucking kidding me," I burst out.

"Everyone at the hospital has been kind. I've read about hospitals that wouldn't have let us anywhere near him. Hospitals that wouldn't accept Brian's medical power of attorney. I heard about one where the staff wouldn't even go into the patients' rooms. They left meals on the floor outside. They didn't care whether people were too ill to get out of bed and get their breakfasts."

"The hospital gets credit for simply not being cruel?"

"Nick," Brian said.

Franklin forged on, "They get credit for treating us like anyone else. They get credit for treating us like Ross' family."

"That's what we are," I said, lamely. Of course, he was right. The hospital *should* get credit for treating Ross and us like anyone else. I was just angry because, well, I was just angry.

Franklin went into the kitchen and came back with plates of Chinese food. I was enormously hungry and completely uninterested in food at the same time. My first bite of General Tso's chicken left me with a dried pepper broken in two on my tongue. It burned. I drank the rest of my second vodka and tonic and asked for a third.

We didn't say much during dinner. Well, I swore about the pepper a few times, but that was about it. Afterward, Franklin took the dishes into the kitchen. I could hear him washing them by hand even though there was a dishwasher.

"Thank you," Brian said.

"What for?"

"You introduced me to Ross. Don't you remember?"

"Yeah, I remember."

And then, as if I'd said I didn't remember at all, he went on, "I had an enormous crush on you. Probably because you'd just saved my life. I showed up on Valentine's Day ready to make you dinner. Ross was there. And you gave me the brush off."

"By instigating a three way. Not my finest hour."

"No, it was perfect. I ended up with Ross because of it. He was still kind of with Earl. And then when Earl died we began spending more time together."

I couldn't help but think that there were so many people in the world who would have cursed me for that introduction. It had very likely led to Brian's having the virus, someday having AIDS. So many people would have hated me for that but not Brian. He thanked me.

More and more I thought life made people more of whatever they were. Brian was good, life made him better. Rita was bad, life made her worse.

"Sugar," I said abruptly.

"What?"

"When is she coming back?"

"The middle of September, I think."

"Shit. There's something I should tell her but I don't think I should do it over the phone."

"Can you tell me?"

I thought for a moment. If there was anyone in Chicago who would keep Gloria's secret it was Brian. So I told him.

"Why does Sugar need to know that? I know she hates Gloria, but I don't think she'll be happy to hear—"

"Sugar said some things to me that—well, her husband may have had sex with Gloria."

"Oh. I see." Brian took a long gulp of his drink. "She invited us up to Charlevoix. I told her no, but I can change my mind. You should come with us. You deserve a vacation."

"I don't think I'm supposed to leave town."

Franklin came in with two pints of Häagen-Dazs, chocolate chip and strawberry. We made short work of them and then drank the rest of the vodka.

————

I HAD TROUBLE SLEEPING. Not at first; at first I was out like a light. But around four in the morning, I woke and began to wonder what the rest of my life was going to be like in prison. And then I wondered if it mattered. Everything felt like it was falling apart. Maybe I should let it. Maybe I should just let whatever was going to happen, happen. Not bother fighting back.

No. I couldn't do that. It might not matter what happened to me, but somewhere there were people who didn't know what had happened to the Jane Doe in the box. She was a daughter, sister, friend. If I went to prison no one who loved her would know what happened to her because officially it would be Rita who I'd killed.

Except Rita, of course. She'd know and she'd be free as a bird flitting around conning new people, blackmailing new people, stealing from new people. I couldn't let that happen.

So I got up and quietly got dressed. Luckily, the Melrose was open twenty-four hours. I got there just after five. I had a bit of a hangover, one that would get worse as I continued to sober up. I needed heavy doses of coffee and bacon to avert that. I ordered the biggest breakfast they had. The day's newspapers sat in front of me, but I wasn't reading them. Not yet.

Joseph. I could have found him the night before and I'd chosen not to. I was beginning to regret that. No, I *did* regret that. Love and sorrow had curled up in my chest like a feral beast. Every so often the beast would hiss and snarl, and I'd ignore it. I knew I couldn't ignore it forever. Sooner or later it had to be dealt with, tamed. Wouldn't finding Joseph accomplish that?

Brian hadn't said anything about him the night before. I believed Brian when he said he couldn't reach him, didn't know where he was. That he had to wait for Joseph to contact him.

Still, maybe I should drop everything and try to find him. I had a good excuse. He might have come home the night that Jane Doe was killed. Maybe he could alibi me. An excuse was all it was though. I didn't think he'd come home that night. I really didn't. I just wanted to find him. To bring him back. I could face my apartment if we were together. Or at least I hoped I could.

After my second cup of coffee I opened the *Daily Herald*. Ignoring the news of the world, I skimmed along until I found an article about the murder. It was on page 7. The headline of the article was "Body in a Box." More information had been released. I skimmed it. They didn't know anything I didn't know. I wondered if I should try contacting the reporter to see if he knew anything he hadn't put in the article. Of course, he'd be trying just as hard to pump me for information in return. Not worth it. Not yet.

Then I remembered that the article on Gunner's death mentioned he lived in Niles. Was that where Rita grew up? Where she went to high school? Did it matter? If Jane Doe was a school friend, yes. That would matter. But was that the best lead I had? I put the idea on the back-burner.

The waitress brought my breakfast and I scarfed it down with the speed of a prison inmate. Ironic, I know. When I walked out of the Melrose it was nearly 6 a.m. The sun was about to come up; the street had turned hazy gray. It was so early there wasn't a lot I could do, though I had a hunch and decided to follow it.

I walked down Broadway, past He Who Eats Mud and the bookstore, the coffee place and the new bakery, the Closet, a half a dozen boutiques that sprang up out of nowhere selling greeting cards and joke T-shirts, sneakers and underwear. When I got to Cornelia I turned toward the lake.

I stopped in front of a twenty-story condominium. There were balconies on each end and angled windows in between so more of the owners could have a view of the lake. It was made of yellow brick and concrete painted white.

I walked into the lobby and asked the doorman if he'd ring Doreen Appleton.

"I will, but she ain't there," he said.

"Oh? Out of town?" I asked, a little afraid she'd run for her life.

"No, she's out jogging."

"Ah," I said. My hunch had been that she'd be up early doing a routine in front of her TV. Running along the lake wasn't that far off. I thanked the doorman and went back out to the street.

I decided to wait on the corner of Cornelia and Lake Shore. The nearest entrance to the park was an underpass at Belmont she'd have gone over to use the dirt path that ran along the lakefront. That particular corner was on her way back home.

It was moments like that I missed smoking the most. Having a cigarette, I would have felt like I was doing something other than just standing there. Sure, it was hardly constructive —in fact it was very *de*structive—but it was something to do. Instead, I stood there with my hands jammed into my jeans staring at the sky feeling like I'd lost a friend.

The sky seemed to be one big oppressive cloud. It would be a hot, humid day. I could feel it already. The air was heavy around me. Sometimes, I felt like Chicago had the worst weather in the world. Too hot, too cold, too windy, too snowy, too humid. It was hard to say why anyone chose to live there.

But then I wondered, *Did I choose to live here?* I'd been born in Chicago and simply stayed. There was a whole big world out there I had never bothered with. Sometimes I wondered if there might be a place I'd like better. Or a place that liked me better.

Doreen Appleton saw me before I saw her. When I noticed her, she'd just stopped running, was huffing and puffing, and the look on her face suggested she was deciding whether to turn and bolt. We looked each other in the eye and she gave up the idea. She was thinner than I remembered, swimming in a pink velour jogging outfit, one that was far more fashionable than functional.

"You again," she said with a gasp. "Are you here to tell me another story?"

"No, I'm—"

"Nick Nowak. I already know that. I read the newspaper. Speaking of which, I'm surprised you're out of jail."

Doreen kept walking. I kept pace with her.

"I made my bond," I said.

"Bill hasn't been that lucky. When you commit financial crimes they get real picky about where the money comes from."

"Are they coming after your condo?"

"They're trying to. But most of the crimes they've accused him of happened after he left me. We're going to court, but my lawyer thinks I'll be able to keep it."

"Good for you."

We were almost in front of her building when she stopped walking. "I'm not going to invite you up. No offense."

"None taken."

"I read about Rita. I really don't think you killed her. But it's not the kind of thing I want to be wrong about, you know?"

"I can see that. Will you answer a few questions?"

"If it doesn't take too long."

"The woman in the box was in her twenties, probably a dishwater blonde, not much in the way of a bosom. She would have been medium height—"

"Wait. That doesn't sound like Rita."

"I don't think it is Rita."

"Shit. Are you sure?"

"The police haven't come to that conclusion. But I have."

"You know, I saw her once. It was the boobs that got me. Bill always said he didn't like big boobs, said more than a mouthful was wasted. Fucking liar."

It was a white lie. Maybe even a kind lie. And if he'd stuck to that kind of lying I wouldn't be standing there with her.

"No one comes to mind?"

She shrugged. "She might have dyed her hair. In fact, she probably did. No one wants to be a dirty blonde. Could have been a lot of people."

"What about a guy? Tall, light hair—"

"Rita has another boyfriend? Already?"

"I don't know much about their relationship."

"I went to see him. My ex-husband. Bill."

"Oh yeah? How was that?"

"He wants me back. Tried to convince me to sell the condo and post his bond. I didn't appreciate that. I don't think he enjoyed the visit."

"You feel better afterwards?"

"Much."

"So the guy who was seen with Rita. He's about six foot four, blue eyes, sandy hair, not much of a chin, eyes close together." She went pale and I knew I was getting somewhere. "You know who I'm talking about?"

Doreen nodded. Just the idea of this guy upset her.

"What's his name?"

"Possum. That's what his friends called him. Mike. Mike Mazur. He was in our wedding."

"He's violent, isn't he?" That wasn't a stretch. There was a dead girl after all.

"A friend of mine dated him a few times, but decided she wasn't really into him. He came to her place, beat her up. Raped her."

"Is he in prison?"

She shook her head. "Kelly—that's my friend—she didn't want to go through all that. I can't blame her. Bill said we'd never see the guy again. Either of us. I guess that's another lie."

"Where did your ex-husband know Mazur from?"

"I think high school. But who knows. He said once Mike did him favors, but he wouldn't say exactly what kind of favors."

"You said he was in your wedding. Do you have a picture?"

"I threw the pictures out. Except the one I showed you last time you were here. And I don't think that one's long for the world."

"All right, thanks. I appreciate—"

"You know what's funny? Going into a marriage things look one way and then coming out of it those same things look completely different."

Chapter Eleven

NOW I HAD A NAME: Mike Mazur. I recognized the surname. There were Mazurs in Bridgeport. He was Polish, like me. I had a decision to make: I could drop everything and go looking for Mike Mazur or I could go on with my day. The thing was, I already knew where Mazur could be located. He was with Rita. I could track down his family members and ask if they knew where to find him, but I doubted they did.

And... I probably knew where he was anyway. It was entirely possible, no, make that probable, that he and Rita were at Marina City. I hadn't been able to get into the building, so I wasn't a hundred percent sure. They could be holed up somewhere else in the city, but my gut said they were there.

It took a little while but I finally remembered that I'd left the Lincoln over by the Belmont El stop. It took an extra twenty minutes to walk there, I was actually closer to the Addison stop. But that didn't matter, it was 7 a.m. on a Saturday morning and there wasn't much I could do. When I found the car, I drove out to Milwaukee Avenue and headed toward Niles.

I stopped at a gas station and got directions to the nearest high school, which turned out to be Niles West. After finding my way to Oakton, I drove to Austin and turned south. The high school was enormous and looked a bit like a factory. There were sprawling parking lots on two sides. Since it was early Saturday morning there were few cars.

I wasn't sure exactly what I was going to do. The offices wouldn't be open, so I didn't know who I might speak to about a student who attended the school… when? When would Rita have been there? I did a little math and figured out she would have been at Niles West sometime in the late sixties to early seventies. This felt like it might be futile.

Next to the school were the athletic fields. There were quite a lot of them. I slowed down and watched for a moment. Their football team was practicing in one of the fields. I parked and got out. Sometimes coaches were also teachers. I wondered if it might be worth talking to any of the adults standing on the sidelines.

But then I noticed that a marching band was rehearsing on the actual football field in front of a set of bleachers. Since bands were coed, I thought I might have better luck down there. I doubted Rita was a band type any more than she was a cheerleader type, but my guess was she was a weird kid and that made band a more likely place to ask about her. She probably didn't play an instrument, but someone might have heard of her.

School hadn't started for the year so, not surprisingly, the band was having a lot of trouble marching and playing their instruments at the same time. When I got down to the field, I noted there were two groups of adults standing on the sidelines and others in the bleachers.

When I got close, I stood for a while listening to the band. After a few moments, I realized they were rehearsing "This Land Is Your Land." Part way through, one of the adults—an older guy with a clipboard—blew a whistle and the band stopped. Several of the other adults ran onto the field. The teenagers split themselves into groups. While everyone was shifting around, I walked over to the clipboard guy.

"Excuse me. Um, my cousin was a student here, in the late sixties, I think, and my family's lost touch. I'd like to find out—"

"You should come back on Monday. Talk to someone in the office. They have all the alumni records."

"I know. But I'm only in town for the weekend. I know it's a long shot."

"What's the name?"

"Rita. Rita Lindquist."

"Late sixties?"

"Yes, I think so."

"You're not sure how old your cousin is?"

"Thirty-three," I guessed.

"That would be class of seventy. Your family lost touch a long time ago?"

"We did."

"I didn't start here until seventy-four." Then he looked over at the adults on the field. "Um, no, our section leaders all started after I did."

"Okay. Well, thanks."

"Like I said, come back on Monday. Talk to Art Livsey. He's the vice principal. Been here since the school opened in fifty-nine."

"Thanks," I said, trying not to seem too disappointed. Although, what I thought I'd find out, I have no idea. I turned and began to walk away.

"Hold on," he said, stopping me. "You know, why don't you talk to Cathy Clough? She's right up there in the bleachers. Her daughter Tia is our second flute. I think Cathy is class of seventy or seventy-one. Somewhere around there."

"Which one is she?"

"Sunglasses, purple scarf."

"Okay, thanks."

I looked over to the bleachers and picked out a woman close to my own age wearing a giant pair of sunglasses—very dark, white plastic—and a purple scarf in her hair. She wore a pressed white blouse without sleeves, a tight pair of khaki shorts and leather sandals.

When I got to her, I said, "Hi. Sorry to bother you. The, uh, bandleader thought you might be able to help me. I'm trying to locate my cousin who was a student here in the late sixties. Rita Lindquist?"

She looked over the edge of her glasses at me. Her eyes were pretty but bloodshot. "You're lying. You're a reporter, aren't you? You guys called a couple of friends of mine."

"Um, busted."

Turning away from me she watched the field.

"Do you remember Rita?" I asked.

"I didn't know her, not really. I haven't talked to her since we were sixteen. And I certainly don't know anything about her murder."

"That's okay. I'm doing a deep background kind of story. I want to let our readers know what kind of person she was."

"Which paper?"

"*Daily Herald*." That seemed to please her, so I marched on. "What kind of kid was Rita?"

"A mess. Her mother died when we were in grade school. We were a year apart, so I knew of her more than knowing her."

The more she told me she didn't know Rita, the more I believed she did.

"It was just her and her father. They had a little house, on Prospect I think. Her dad wasn't there much. The house was disgusting. Dirty dishes everywhere. Weeks old. Just gross. But that didn't stop us from hanging out there. You know, kids."

"Did you hang out there a lot?"

"No. A couple of months maybe. During my stoner phase. My very brief stoner phase."

"Did she have any other relatives? A cousin, maybe, someone who was a bit younger than her?" I asked. It hadn't occurred to me before, but the girl in the box could be related to her.

Cathy shook her head. "I mean she might have had cousins or whatever. She stopped coming to school before she was even seventeen. So, you know, I lost contact."

"Did something happen? Was there a reason she stopped coming to school?"

Cathy shrugged. "Probably. But we were kids. If we didn't

know what was happening we just made it up. There were rumors, but I don't think any of them were true."

"What kind of rumors?"

"That she'd had a baby and gotten married, that she'd gotten arrested, that she joined some Christian choir touring the country. It was ridiculous."

"Didn't you ever just go by her house to find out?"

"I think I did once, but she wasn't there." Then she looked at me very seriously. "Do you really think any of this had to do with her getting murdered?"

"Probably not," I said. "It does paint kind of a sad picture, though. Well, thank you."

I began to walk away. As I did, she said, "It said in the newspaper that she took over her dad's business. That she was a private eye. When we were kids she'd tell us she worked with him. We didn't believe her, but now I wonder. She was kind of weird about her dad too."

I nodded. "I've heard that before."

———

I DROVE BACK into the city, found a parking space near Brian's, and then walked over to the Belmont El station. After a ten-minute wait, I took the Ravenswood down to the Merchandise Mart stop. Then I walked across the river and down to 333 Wacker. It was a teal glass tower that reflected the gray sky, except when the building was done the sky wasn't gray anymore. It was a steel blue, the kind of color a decorator might call bold and determined.

I walked into the green marble lobby and went right over to the onyx-and-chrome security desk. When I'd been before it was during the week, so I'd simply carried an envelope and acted like I belonged. That wasn't going to work this time. It was too empty to get away with it. I was going to have to try something else.

The guard was a black woman in her fifties. She looked pissed off. I didn't think I was going to make things any better.

"Can I help you?"

"Yeah, I have a meeting at Carney, Greenbaum and Turner."

"With whom?"

"Oh, you know, I left the card in my other jeans."

"Did you. I can't let you up there if you don't know who it is you want to see."

"Well, he's a lawyer."

"That doesn't narrow it down."

"Maybe you could just call up there."

She looked at me for a moment; looking for the path of least resistance, I think. When she found it, she said, "Fine. What's your name?"

I decided I'd use the same gambit I'd used on Gloria except with a twist. "Rita Lindquist."

"You don't look like any Rita Lindquist."

"It's probably the way the light's catching my face."

"That's not funny," she deadpanned and then, after a long moment, added, "You know what's funny? I forgot my lunch money."

I took a twenty out of my wallet and handed it to her. She crumbled it up in her palm, picked up the phone and dialed. After a moment someone answered. "I have a Rita Lindquist here."

She waited. Then she said, "All right. Thank you." She hung up the phone and said, "They're on the fourteenth floor. But you probably already know that."

"I do. Thank you. Enjoy your lunch."

"You have a nice day, Rita."

I took the elevator up to the fourteenth floor. When the doors opened a man around my own age was standing there, waiting. He was heavy around the middle, wore an expensive pair of khakis and pink button-down, and he was sweating. Profusely.

I stepped out of the elevator.

"You're not Rita," he said in a sigh.

"I'm not. But I'm here to talk about her."

"That's not really—"

A young woman in her twenties, also casually dressed with a cardigan sweater wrapped around her, came out of the double doors that bore the name of the firm. She crossed the lobby to the blank set of doors on the other side. As she walked by, she said, "Tommy, I'll be ready to sit down in a half an hour." With a glance to me she added, "If you're free."

"I'll be free."

When she was completely gone, he said, "Follow me." We went through the double doors into a bigger lobby, then worked our way around until we got to one of the large, outer offices. The design of the building was clever. There weren't really any corner offices, so it wasn't immediately apparent who was important and who wasn't. Although, Tommy's office was expensively decorated, so it was obvious that he was a big deal.

"So, who are you?" I asked.

"Tommy Carney," he said, sitting down behind his large mahogany desk. At the edge of his desk, right in front of me was a collection of autographed golf balls. That meant something to me, but I couldn't think what just then. I shook the thought off—

"So, you're a partner? Here on a Saturday?"

"It's my father's name on the door. I'm a junior. And a junior partner. I have to try harder, no matter what. The better question is who are you?"

"Nick Nowak. I'm the man accused of murdering Rita."

"You want us to defend you?"

"I have a lawyer."

"Then why are you here?"

"618 North Wells."

He took a clean, pressed handkerchief out of his desk drawer and mopped his forehead. It needed it.

"Anything I know about that property is privileged."

"That's not entirely true. You're required to report crimes if you know of them."

"If I know of them in advance. I can assure you I don't know of any upcoming crimes."

"So you knew nothing of Gunner Lindquist's death in advance of its happening?"

"No."

I had the feeling that was a lie. Or at least a half-truth.

"How did Rita Lindquist come to work for you?"

"We had a contract with Gunner's firm. When he died, Rita was basically the firm. We really had no choice in the matter."

"And you couldn't find a legal loophole?"

"You're a private investigator, aren't you? Are you trying to get our account? That's pretty bold since you might be in prison soon."

I sat very still. My gut said he knew something about Gunner Lindquist's death, but then they took on his daughter as his replacement. Was that to deter suspicion? Or did they really have no choice?

"Rita's not dead," I said.

Tommy's face turned a putty color and looked like it might slide off the bone. "What does that mean? It was in the paper—"

"It's another girl in the box. Think about it. The only real reason to cut off someone's head and hands is to prevent identification. It's not Rita."

"Shit," he said. It was a very small sound.

"The murdered woman is between twenty-five and thirty, medium-sized, dishwater blonde hair—possibly dyed, small breasts. Do you know anyone fitting that description connected to Rita?"

He shook his head.

"Do you know who Mike Mazur is? Nickname Possum."

"Yeah, I know who he is. A friend of Rita's boyfriend. We got him out of a little scrape."

"Rape? You mean rape, don't you?"

"It was a misunderstanding."

"Was he charged?"

"Is that important?"

It was actually. If the police already knew him, this got

easier. "When a lawyer answers a question with a question it usually means I'm onto something."

"Or it means nothing."

He dabbed his face again with the handkerchief. His forehead, his cheeks, his neck. That meant something. That meant a lot of something.

"It's cold in here," I said. "Frigid actually."

"It saves money to run the air conditioning at a steady temperature. When the full staff is here it's considerably warmer. Body heat."

"You're sweating, though. Something about this conversation is making you nervous."

"Everything about Rita Lindquist makes me nervous."

"Have you had contact with her in the last few months?"

"I can't talk about that."

"That's a yes. Did she threaten you?"

"I can't talk about that."

I nodded. "Look, I'm trying to find Rita. If I find her, your problems go away. Can you tell me anything?"

He sweat some more while he thought. "Her payroll checks go to a P.O. box in Niles."

"Wait. You're still paying her?"

"It seemed like a good idea."

"And you don't want to poke the beast."

———

I LEFT A FEW MINUTES LATER, after he'd given me everything he was going to. Tommy Junior said checks went out on Monday every week. Rita's check wouldn't be there until maybe Tuesday. I could go out to Niles and watch the post office until she showed up. Unless, of course, I was back in County. Then I wasn't watching anything.

I walked back over to the El and got on it thinking I'd get off at Belmont and stop at Brian's. Instead, I jumped off at Armitage and took a very long walk over to Hudson. More than a dozen blocks, almost half an hour. In my head, I went over everything Tommy Carney Junior told me or didn't tell me. He was scared and that meant Rita had something on him or on the firm. Or she might have threatened Tommy's kids the way she did Jill Smith's.

I had the feeling Tommy's fear of Rita went back to her father's death. They must have tried to get rid of her and it was then that she'd forced her way into a job. A job she didn't even have to go to for them to pay her.

And what was the deal with the golf balls? Why did they seem important to me? They weren't. Obviously, they weren't. The fact that Tommy Carney, Jr., liked to collect Jack Nicklaus' balls didn't mean anything. So why did I think it did?

Then I was back on Andrew Happ's street. I'd only talked to one of his neighbors so far. She'd liked Ruby, as she called her, and didn't want to believe anything bad about her. I could use another opinion.

Directly across the street from Happ's was a yellow brick apartment building. I skipped that. Renters never talked to each other the way owners did. It was entirely possible that none of them knew anything about Rita or Andrew Happ. Instead I went to the house just north of that building. It was a little distant from Happ's house, so I didn't expect much.

I knocked on the door of the painted brick house, three stories like the others. After a bit, a woman answered the door. She was in her early thirties and she'd obviously just hurried through the big house to get to the front door. A seven- or eight-year-old boy was clinging to her.

"Hi, can I help you?" she asked when she opened the door.

"I'm an investigator," I started. When you drop the private people often assumed you were a police officer; a distinct advantage. "Did you know your neighbor, Andrew Happ?"

"The old man who died recently? Not well. I have a job at J. Walter, so I'm not here much during the week."

"I see. And what about his niece, Ruby? Did you ever meet her?"

She shook her head.

The little boy looked up at me and asked, "Can I have your pennies?"

"Leo, we've talked about this. You don't ask strangers for their pennies." She looked at me and said, "I'm sorry."

"No, that's fine," I said, digging into my pocket for change. "What about a young woman, not too tall, dirty blonde hair, not very chesty. You see anyone like that around?"

"No. When I'm home this one keeps me busy, so I don't have a lot of time to notice my neighbors."

I nodded, then said to Leo, "I've only got two pennies. How about a nickel and a dime?"

The boy shook his head violently.

"He collects pennies," his mother said. "He's looking for ones from the war—42, 43. They were steel rather than copper. They're collectible."

"I see. The war was a really long time ago," I said as I handed Leo my two pennies. And as I did, it hit me. Coins. Collecting coins. I'd been in Happ's house the week before. I remembered looking at his bookcase. He had a collector's guide to U.S. coins and big empty space next to it. Rita had taken the man's coin collection.

"Nineteen sixty-five, nineteen seventy-two," he said, disappointment in his voice.

"You know, Mr. Happ collected coins."

"Really? Small world."

"Do you have a phone book?" I asked.

"Of course," she said, a bit confused. "You want to look at the phone book?"

"Yellow pages."

"All right." She stepped away from the door, pulling the boy with her. A minute or so later she was back, this time without the boy. Chicago was big enough that we had white pages and yellow pages in two different directories. I took the yellow pages out of her hands and flipped it open, turning the pages until I found what I wanted. RARE COIN DEALERS. I ripped the page out of the book and handed it back to her.

"Um, what—"

"Thanks," I said, heading down the stoop to the sidewalk. I walked the three blocks over to Clark and found a bus stop. The bus arrived about four minutes later. I got on, found a seat in the back, and began to study my list. I put them in a kind of order, figuring out what would be the most efficient way to approach this.

Yes, I could have gone to my office and simply called all the places, but I like to see people when I talk to them. It's easier to figure out if they're lying or holding something back. Plus, my office was a disaster I never wanted to look at again.

I jumped off the bus at Belmont and walked around until I found my car on Elaine Place. It was after eleven. Time flies when your freedom's on the line. I spent the next three hours going from coin dealer to coin dealer. I went to six of them and finally got lucky with number seven.

The place was called Willoughby Coins & Stamps. It was up in Edgewater on Ridge. A little white brick building with tiny windows that suggested they didn't want anyone to know too much about what was going on inside. When I walked in I saw that it was a very small space, smaller than the building suggested. There were a couple of glass cases displaying the stamps and coins for sale. For some reason I had the feeling Willoughby bought more coins than he sold. Which made me wonder what might be happening to them.

An older gentleman sat behind one of the glass cases reading *The Reader*. His hair was gray and his skin chalky. He glanced at me when I walked in. Since I wasn't holding anything to sell, he said, "Go ahead, look around. You want something particular you just say so. I might got it in the back or maybe can get it for you."

I introduced myself and gave him my card. Which reminded me, maybe I ought to check my messages once in a while. I worried about that while he studied the card. Then he said, "Okay, what do you want? Everything I do is legit. I don't fence. Never"

"I'm looking for a woman, early thirties, red-hair, a chest you'd remember. Might have been with a guy, six-four, blond hair, blue eyes, no chin, nickname Possum. Looks like his nickname. They'd have been selling several random collections of U.S. coins."

He was silent for a bit, like he wasn't going to answer me, but then he did. "Yeah, they was in here. Last Tuesday, maybe. I offered her a price for all of it and she got mad as a hornet. Least-wise she tried to. I got the impression I weren't their first stop."

"Did you buy the coins?"

"Most of it was crap. But there was a couple steel pennies, a Buffalo head nickel in bad shape, a few liberty dollars. Most people don't understand. You don't just put a coin in a drawer, wait twenty years and then, bam, it's worth something. Usually, there has to be something wrong with it. Something what makes it unique."

As he talked, something clicked for me. Rita had expected to get a lot more for the coins. She thought they'd be able to get by on whatever she got for them. When that proved wrong, she had Possum go in and get some money from Winslow Porter's account.

"Did she sell the coins to you?"

"She did. She didn't want to, but she did."

"Did you write a check?"

"She wanted cash. I don't do cash, I write checks. That way I got a record."

"So you got her name?"

"Yes, finally she took a check."

"Uh-huh, what name did she give you?"

He eyed me suspiciously. "Not sure I can say."

That seemed odd. He'd said a lot already.

"The thing is, those coins were stolen. So you can give me her name, which will send me off looking for her. Or I can leave empty handed, giving me plenty of time to call the police and let them know you've got some stolen coins for sale."

With a dirty look, he reached under the counter and pulled out a fistful of yellow carbons. Each was a copy of a handwritten receipt. He dug through them, pulled one out and read, "Hillary Buckman."

My first thought was how odd that was. Rita always used names that had her initials. Made up names. So did that mean this wasn't made up?

The address on the receipt was 618 North Wells. Then, I remembered there were Buckmans on the board there, personal friends of Gloria Silver. They must have a daughter named Hillary, a daughter who was very likely the girl in the box. And I was going to have to let them know.

Chapter Twelve

IT WAS the middle of the afternoon and I hadn't eaten. I drove back to Boystown and parked around the corner from a gyros place on Broadway. I got the special: a gyros wrapped in foil and an order of thick, greasy fries. Then I headed back to Brian's. No one was home, so I spread my lunch out on the big dining room table, grabbed a pop from the kitchen, then went and got his cordless phone, pulling the antenna out fully.

Taking a giant bite of my sandwich, I dialed the number for the *Daily Herald*. I was still chewing when Gloria answered.

"Hello. Hello?"

I hadn't actually expected her to answer. I thought I'd have to listen to a message first, giving me time to finish chewing.

"Uh—"

"Who is this?"

I swallowed. "It's Nick."

"Oh," she said, clearly not happy. "Look, I've hardly had any time to do what you asked. I had three events last night that I just had to go to… and I have two tonight. I'll be able to spend some time on this Monday after I turn in my column."

"Hillary Buckman."

"What about her?"

"I've connected her to Rita. She might be the girl in the box."

"No. You're wrong. Hilly used to come to our house for sleepovers. She's friends with my daughter."

I decided not to mention that childhood sleepovers were no protection from murder.

"When was the last time you saw the Buckmans?" I asked.

"I saw Diane last night at a function."

"How did she seem?"

"Fine. You don't think they know, do you?"

"They could."

"They *couldn't*. They'd do something."

"How old is the girl?"

"Twenty, twenty-one."

"So she's old enough to go where she pleases without telling her parents."

"Yes, but—"

"That's what the police would say. So even if the Buckmans called them, no one's really looking for the girl."

"Oh my God."

"Gloria, I need to talk to your friends."

The line went silent.

"I'm seeing them tonight at the Susan Wollinger Cancer Research Dinner. I'll ask—"

"Can I come?" I asked. There was a little urgency here, after all.

"What are you going to say to them? You can't tell them their daughter is dead in the middle of a black-tie dinner."

"I don't know their daughter's dead. I only think she might be. Maybe they'll say they've heard from her. Really, this needs to happen soon."

She was silent a moment. "I don't suppose you have anything appropriate to wear?"

"No. Can you bring them outside? Can I meet you afterward? Or before? Before would be better."

"That would terrify them. Hold on a moment."

She put me on hold. Suddenly, I was listening to Muzak. "Close to You," not sung by The Carpenters. Gloria was right, of course. I had to find a way to get information from the Buckmans without terrifying them. The minute they thought their daughter was dead they'd be useless.

Gloria came back on the line. "Meet me at Walton Richards on Michigan. It's on the ground floor of The Allerton. Five-thirty. Don't be late, they're staying open just for us. And... please be freshly showered and well-shaved."

Then she hung up on me. I wanted to be annoyed with her about that remark, but I have to say I didn't always bother—at least with the shaving part. I read the time off the VCR: 4:05. I had a little bit of time, so I decided to check in with my attorney.

I called Owen at home, but when his answering machine answered I hung up. Then I tried him at his office.

"Yes?" he said, picking up the phone.

"It's Nick."

"Hello, darling. What have you been doing?"

"I think the girl in the box is Hillary Buckman. Rita's been using her identity and the girl is related to a couple on the board of 618 North Wells."

"Be careful, Nick. There are a lot of bad people connected to that address."

"One of whom had Rita's father killed. I think she may be getting her revenge."

"That's probably true. If we can find another way at this we should probably take it."

I was beginning to have the feeling he knew more than he was saying about the unfinished building. I could have asked him, but I knew he wouldn't tell me.

"The autopsy says the girl is twenty-five to thirty. This girl is twenty. Can they be that wrong?"

"Absolutely. And they often are."

"I'm going to talk to the parents tonight. Gloria Silver is taking me to a black-tie dinner."

"Somebody's going to have an unpleasant evening." I wasn't entirely sure whether he meant them or me.

"Rita's accomplice is named Mike Mazur, also known as

Possum. He was in Bill Appleton's wedding, but later raped a friend of his wife's."

"Charming."

"I think he may be the one who actually killed Hillary."

"Makes sense."

"There weren't any indications of rape, were there? Can you call the medical examiner and ask?"

"No, I can't call Padma. I got an earful for going around the ASA. I'll have to call Tony Stork."

"Can you reach him on Saturday?"

"Of course, I have his home number."

"Do you?"

"You have a filthy mind. Anyway—I've been making calls. Steven Head has been a snitch before, which is perfect. A jury might believe he heard one jailhouse confession but not two."

"Especially if you crush him like a bug on the stand."

"I won't be doing the cross-exam," he said. Of course, I knew that. The firm he worked for wouldn't put him in front of a jury. He was too gay. It was very likely they'd hold that against him. Someone else from his firm would lead at trial. Someone less, well, less Owen.

He went on. "I'll also remind Tony that Rita is not the only one who knows his secrets."

"You're going to blackmail him? Isn't that unethical?"

"Darling, if my sensibilities were *that* delicate all my clients would be in prison and no one would ever pay me."

I wasn't sure how I felt about that, so I said, "I have to get ready."

"Call me tomorrow and tell me everything," he said, as though we were just two gossipy friends and not a lawyer and his client.

―――――

WHEN I GOT out of the shower, all clean and carefully shaved, I heard someone in the apartment. Wearing a towel, I came out of the bathroom and said, "Hello."

"Hi," Brian said.

Something in that tiny word made me ask, "What's going on?"

He shook his head. "I've been with Ross, that's all. They gave him a lot of drugs. It helps with the breathing tube, but he's not very aware—"

"That doesn't sound like a bad thing."

"You need to see him."

"I know. It's just—"

"You're in a lot of trouble," Brian said. "I've told him, so I think he knows why you're not there. But still—"

"I'll get over there tomorrow."

"Thank you." I started to walk away, but he said, "Oh, and I talked to Sugar. We're going up to Charlevoix next weekend. And she definitely didn't pay your bond. But she says if you need anything to just call."

"Okay, thanks."

Who did pay my bond then? It was a lot of money and I had very few friends who could have comfortably paid it. If it wasn't Sugar, then who was it? That left me with an uncomfortable feeling, but I still had to get ready to go out.

"And Joseph came by the hospital," Brian added.

"He did?"

"He didn't come home at all on Saturday night."

"So you told him what was happening with me?"

"I did. He said he'd pray for you."

"Pray for me? That's what he said?"

"Yes."

"Fuck him."

"Nick."

"I have to get dressed."

In the bedroom, I threw on some clothes. I was running late. Ten minutes later I was in a cab on my way to Michigan Avenue. Pray for me? Really? I was in trouble and that's what he was willing to do for me? If he were in trouble I'd be doing everything—

No, I was wrong. He *was* in trouble and I wasn't doing

anything for him. Sure, that's what he wanted. He wanted me to leave him alone and for some reason, and I wasn't entirely sure why, I was doing that.

For a few miles, I thought about how things might be if there hadn't been a body in box outside my office, if I hadn't been arrested, if I weren't facing the prospect of spending my life in prison. What would this week have been? Well, it would have been shitty. I probably would have roused myself and started looking for Joseph. And when I found him, what would have happened? Was he with this Alejandro person now? Or had he gone back to the church?

And could I compete with either of them? Sometimes I felt like a chasm had opened between us and there was no way for me to cross it. Other times I felt like I'd fallen into that same chasm, never to find my way out.

Walton Richards looked like it was doing an imitation of some hoity-toity British tailor and since they'd had Est. 1959 painted on the window in gold leaf they were apparently doing a good job of it. When I opened the front door, I immediately saw Gloria Silver in a puffy peach dress that made her look a bit like a straw shoved into a cupcake. Next to her was a severe looking woman in her mid-fifties with flat black hair cut chin length with bangs. That woman, who was very short, wore a pair of out-of-fashion platform shoes with a lemon-colored gown. The gown was too tight, showing off her lumps, with a frayed and dirty hem that had obviously been stepped on. Around her shoulders was a white fox stole—unnecessary, as it was near eighty degrees and unlikely to plunge into the forties overnight.

"Nick. There you are. Cyril just went to get a couple of tuxes for us to look at. This is Adelaide Summers, fashion editor for the *Daily Herald*.

"Hello," I said, thinking this must explain why the woman looked so ridiculous. I smiled at Adelaide. She grimaced back. To Gloria I said, "Cyril? Is that for real?"

"He's probably Chuck from Cicero, but be nice and call him Cyril."

"Got it."

"You aren't really a private investigator, are you?" Adelaide said. "I thought they disappeared with Studebakers."

"I guess I'm a Studebaker then."

One side of Adelaide's mouth went up and I decided to call it a smile.

"Why does it matter what I look like, anyway?" I asked. "I'm not expecting to stay all night at this thing."

"You're going to be standing next to me," Gloria said. "You need to look good. You may not have a reputation to uphold, but I do."

Cyril came out from a stock room. He was a dumpy guy in his late fifties with an Irish nose and a permanent blush in his cheeks. He held a pair of tuxedos on hangers. One in each hand.

"Oh, the one on the right," Adelaide said.

"Yes, absolutely," Gloria agreed.

Honestly, I couldn't tell the difference between them. They were both black with wide lapels.

Cyril assessed me. "Hmmmm, 42L, I think. I'll be right back." But first he pulled at the waist of my jeans for a second. I nearly slapped him. "Smaller in the waist."

He scurried off.

To Gloria, I said, "Wouldn't this have been easier if we just met your friends for a drink before the event?"

She rolled her eyes. "It's a charity. For cancer. We're not upsetting the Buckmans until they've written their check. Besides, I've already had my daughter make a few calls. I told you they were friends... well, apparently Hilly has made new friends and has been dropping all her old ones. And to top it off, she's in love."

"With Possum," I guessed.

"Apparently. Although I think it's ridiculous. No woman could love a man named Possum."

"Any woman who marries a grown man with a nickname is a fool," the fashion director added.

"Adelaide!" Gloria said, "I might need to steal that."

"Consider it yours."

Cyril came back with a tux, a crisp white shirt and a box of studs. Then he led me to a changing room that was nearly as large as my apartment. He hung the tux on a hook and handed me a plastic bag with the Walton Richards logo on it.

"What's this for?"

"Your clothes," he said, trying to give his Chicago accent an upper class spin. "I'm told you're going directly to the event."

He walked out and I stared at the bag. People were giving me plastic bags to put my clothes in a lot lately. I started to change.

Did I really need to go to this thing? I was pretty sure the girl in the box was Hillary Buckman and that Mike "Possum" Mazur had killed her, possibly at Rita's instruction. Unfortunately, it didn't seem like being "pretty sure" about anything was going to get me out of trouble.

I was also pretty sure Rita and Possum were hiding out at Marina City. But I couldn't prove it and I wasn't sure I could weasel my way into the building. And if I did… well, my guns had been taken in evidence. Rita still had hers. I didn't relish the idea of being shot at again.

I had the tuxedo on. My T-shirt and jeans were crammed into the bag. The suit fit well. Cyril wasn't bad at guessing my size. I went back out into the store so they could all stare at me.

Gloria and Adelaide were talking about whether Jane Byrne would be at the dinner. There were rumors about her challenging the new mayor in the primary, even though that was almost two years off. Cyril came over and began checking the tuxedo's fit.

"It's close enough," I said. He ignored me and put a pin into the waistband. Then he went to get a cummerbund and bow tie. I subtly slipped the pin out and dropped it on the floor.

"I think the mayor *is* coming… she'd have a lot of nerve—" Adelaide was saying.

I interrupted. "Gloria, we don't have much time, could you tell me more about the Buckmans?"

"They're a lovely couple. Mid-fifties, good people really.

They had a tough time during the recession of eighty-two. Elliot made a number of bad investments. At first they thought 618 was a godsend. It didn't turn out that way."

"If they're broke then what are they doing going to an expensive shindig like this?"

"You don't have any idea how money is made, do you?"

In all honesty, I didn't.

"It's never hard to make money when you're in the room with the right people," Adelaide explained. "The challenge in life is getting into that room."

"Oh, I need to steal that too," Gloria said.

"That one you can't have. We don't want the riff-raff figuring out how things are done."

Cyril came back with two sets of cummerbunds and ties. One set was brilliant red, the other a silvery gray. The women studied them closely.

"I don't know, Gloria, don't you think they should be black? He's going to stand out like a peacock in either of these."

"A little attention won't hurt."

"You want everyone to know you're there with a suspected murderer, don't you?" Adelaide asked, then said to me, "She has an innate sense of the dramatic."

Gloria just smiled. It seemed ridiculous that my trouble should somehow raise Gloria's social status, but apparently it did. Gloria turned to Cyril and said, "The red, I think. Now, shoes…" Looking down at the white athletic socks I was wearing, she added, "And socks, of course."

I suppose I should be glad I got to keep my underwear.

Cyril didn't budge. To Adelaide he said, "So there will be a write-up right before the holidays and another the week of New Year's?"

"Yes, of course," Adelaide said. "You'll get your money's worth, ten times over. And he's not keeping the tux, he'll bring everything back on Monday."

Not that anyone had cleared that with me

"Cleaned?"

"Of course," Adelaide promised for me.

"If it has to go to the cleaner, it's not coming back on Monday," I said. That should have been obvious to everyone.

"All right, just bring it back then," Cyril said. "Just don't get anything on it."

"I'll try not to sweat."

"Do," Cyril replied.

Chapter Thirteen

THE GOLD COAST ballroom at the Drake was about the size of a football field spread beneath a dozen king-sized chandeliers. Everything in the room was gold: the columns, the folding chairs the tablecloths, the drapes, the curtain behind the raised stage, even the floral arrangements had been sprayed with gilt. Right as we entered the room there was a table where a woman sat with a legal-sized clipboard and a walkie-talkie.

"Gloria Silver."

"Yes, I know," the woman said, and nearly giggled. Her cheeks turned red, as she marked her clipboard.

"Adelaide Summers."

"Oh my," the woman made another mark on her clipboard then looked up at me. Obviously, she read the *Daily Herald.* "And you are, sir?"

"He's with me," Gloria said. And that settled that.

Abruptly, a woman rushed over. She had a thick head of white hair and wore an ice-blue satin dress with an enormous skirt. "Gloria!" she nearly shouted. "You're so early!"

"I know! I'm so sorry, but I've got another event later on."

"Oh, but you have to stay through dessert. Crème brûlée. We had to hire three extra cooks just to burn the tops."

"I just might. I adore crème brûlée," Gloria said.

"Is the bar open?" Adelaide asked.

"Let's walk over and open it!" As we began to move, she turned to me and said, "We haven't met, I'm Helena Darwin. And you are?"

"Helena this is Nick Nowak, alleged murderer as we say in the press," Gloria introduced me.

"Hello," I said. What else was I going to say?

"Gloria, you are such a kidder." To me she added, "She loves it when people think she's just the slightest bit dangerous."

"I'd say she's very dangerous."

Helena burst out laughing. To Gloria she said, "He's a kidder, isn't he? No really, who are you?"

"I'm a private investigator."

"Like Magnum P.I.!"

"My Ferrari is outside."

That made her titter. We reached the bar, which was a tall table draped in the same gold fabric that covered the dining tables. There was only top shelf liquor and what looked like quality wine.

"Can you make a martini?" Adelaide asked the very attractive bartender.

"Um, sure."

"Vodka. Twist."

As he reached for a rocks glass, I could tell he didn't know what he was doing. "You don't have any up glasses, do you?" I asked.

"No. I mean, I don't think so."

"Oh my God!" Helena blurted. "We should get some then."

"That's fine. I'll have it on the rocks," Adelaide said. "Extra dry, please."

The guy filled a glass with ice. Then he reached for the Vermouth.

"Don't touch the Vermouth," I said. I was right. He didn't have much experience. A seasoned bartender knew that an extra dry vodka martini was simply vodka on the rocks. "I'll have a vodka and soda water when you're finished."

"Glenfiddich and water," Gloria said.

Once we got our drinks, Gloria set hers down and began to

dig around in her clutch. She pulled out a pack of Virginia Slims. I was on the verge of asking to bum one, when she said, "I'm curious, did you ever figure out what Sugar's secret is?"

She'd mentioned something about that to me around Christmas—and not in a nice way.

"No. And I don't care. Secrets have a way of ruining friendships. And I like Sugar."

Then she leaned over and told me the secret anyway. "She was never really a Pilson."

"What does that mean?" Okay, I couldn't help myself.

"That side of the Pilson family, apparently the grandmother, had a dalliance so none of them are truly Pilsons."

"That doesn't seem like such a big secret."

"The money. They're not entitled to it. Not a penny. My guess is Sugar's ex got drunk one night and told her."

Adelaide turned around holding her drink in two hands. She took a sip. "This is wonderful."

"How did you hear this story about Sugar?"

"Rita. She does occasionally get the goods."

"Why haven't you printed it?"

"Sugar's too valuable. People love it every time I write something bitchy about her."

Something from the past came to the forefront. "And she has something on you, doesn't she?"

"And so do you. But I doubt either of you will ever use it, you're both too nice." The way she said the word 'nice' made it clear she wasn't paying us a compliment.

I considered what had just been said. Sugar already knew about Gloria's illness. Good. That meant Brian didn't have to tell her. It also meant I didn't have to. I thought about asking how or why or what, but instead noticed Beverly Harland coming into the room. She wore a shiny black gown and stumbled on her hem.

"Someone's drinking again," Gloria said.

"I can't really blame her. Did you hear what happened to her son?" Adelaide asked.

"No, what happened to her son?"

"Down at Stateville. Beaten. Almost to death. And God knows what else."

"He doesn't belong in a maximum security facility," I said. "He's not violent."

Gloria turned to me and said, "He murdered his stepfather. The man died just feet from me."

I nodded. "I worked the case for Jimmy English."

"Terrible having your son kill your husband," Adelaide said.

"It's the daughter who belongs in prison," I pointed out. "She tricked her brother into it."

"Did she really? How?" Adelaide wanted to know.

I'd said too much. Just because Jimmy English was dead didn't mean it was safe to gossip about his family.

"I really shouldn't say any more."

"Don't worry," Adelaide said. "If I pour enough drinks into Beverly she'll tell me everything." And with that she propelled herself across the room.

People were entering the ballroom at a much faster clip now. Waiters had begun to float around with trays of appetizers. Caviar on tiny bits of toast and that sort of thing.

Soon ASA Sanchez walked in alone. Wearing a tailored charcoal gray suit, she looked like she'd just come there from work and that might even have been true. I had the feeling she was working her way up to running for office, possibly State's Attorney. Maybe even mayor. The more people she locked up the better her chances of winning.

Given what Gloria and Adelaide were talking about earlier, that Jane Byrne might run again, her chances would be improved. Byrne was a divisive figure and so was Washington. Sanchez could present herself as the healing solution.

Gloria leaned over and said, discretely, "Richard Crisp just walked in."

I looked over and saw an older, short man with thinning hair dyed a rosy peach. Next to him was a tall, elegant woman about twenty years younger.

"Is that his wife?"

"No, that's Elaine Kelso," Gloria explained. "She runs a very elite escort service. No one has ever figured out if Richard hires her per event or if he actually owns the service. And by extension, her."

"Either way, people love it when the two of them show up," I supposed. "Should we go over and say hello?"

"God no."

"Why not?" I asked.

"What do you think you're going to say to him?"

"I'm going to ask if he's seen Rita Lindquist."

"A dead woman?"

"She's not—"

"I believe you, but will he? And besides, he'll want to know why you're asking. And you can't say because he killed Rita's father."

"You acted like it's public knowledge," I said, half to tease her.

"Yes, but you can't actually discuss it with the murderer." I'm sure that was somewhere in Emily Post.

I looked back at him. He had to be near seventy. I doubted he actually killed anyone himself. I wondered who he paid to do it.

"You said he had Rita's father killed. If she's taking revenge on the Buckmans for their part, I can't imagine why she wouldn't go after him. Particularly if he's the one who's responsible."

"Richard doesn't have any children," Gloria said. "Or anyone he cares about, for that matter."

"What about secrets?"

"Aside from the fact that he's a con artist and a murderer, none that I know of."

"Everything else does pale in comparison," I admitted.

Deanna Hansen walked in with a tall, good-looking guy not far from her own age. Apparently, she'd dumped the older restaurateur she'd been seeing up until last year. Helena appeared from nowhere and attached herself to the couple. I wondered if people knew who Deanna was and where her money came from. But then I laughed at myself. It didn't matter to this crowd. They despised the mugger, the streetwalker, the welfare cheat, but they revered anyone who knew how to steal big. It never mattered to them where you got your money from or how you got it, as long as you had a lot of it. Helena knew exactly how Deanna made whatever donation she'd be giving. And she didn't care.

"They're here," Gloria said, abruptly.

"Who's here?" I asked.

"My friends." Her voice was layered with gloom and doom. She pulled me in the opposite direction.

"What are you doing?" I asked Gloria.

"I told you. Not until they write their check."

"Gloria!" a woman called out and hurried over. With her, came a cloud of dusty, sweet perfume. I nearly gagged.

As a way of deflecting her, Gloria said, "Nick, do you know Dori Pilson? Sugar's former sister in-law?"

"Actually, I don't."

"Nick is a friend of Sugar's," she said, though it hardly sounded like a recommendation. Dori Pilson held out her hand so I shook it.

"Lovely party, and it's for a good cause. Is Sugar here?"

"No," I said. "She's in Michigan somewhere."

"Charlevoix. That house was in our family for nearly a century."

What was I supposed to do with that? Offer my condolences? It did imply the story Gloria had told me was true. I smiled and said, "This seems like the event of the year. I'm surprised Sugar is missing it."

"Oh it's hardly that," Dori said. "I think the masquerade ball for the Art Institute is a much more exciting event. What do you think, Gloria?"

"I think it's time to find our table. You know at one of these things, years ago, one of the guests started moving the place cards around creating some truly horrific combinations."

"But that would be such a fun thing to put into one of your columns," I pointed out.

"All right, it was me who changed the cards. Don't tell."

A waiter came by and we all sampled a salmon concoction on Melba toast. He told us what it was called, but I immediately forgot. When he wandered off, I said to Gloria "Do you even know where our table is?"

"That way," she said, waving an arm at all the tables. We started to move, which I hoped meant she'd be getting more specific. She leaned in to me and said, "People seem put out by my being with you."

I hadn't seen any indication of that, but still said, "I can't imagine why."

"I'm sure they think I'm screwing you. Such a double standard. A man can date any young thing he wants, but when a woman does it it's somehow disgusting."

"No offense, but you're not going to be my girlfriend."

"Well, of course not. Don't be ridiculous—Oh, here's our table."

We were in the center of the room, very far from the front. Gloria stood a little straighter—hard to tell, as she was buried in flounces, but she managed. Then she waved the Buckmans over.

They were small and a little chubby. They both dyed their hair a shade too dark and spent too little time in the sun. He was dressed in a dusty tux, while she wore a sheath dress that was unflattering and years out of style.

"Elliot! Diane!" Gloria called out to get their attention. They immediately walked over and huddled around Gloria. Diane kissed her on the cheek. "I want you to meet a fr—someone I know. Nick Nowak."

They said hello to me. Elliot held out a hand for me to shake. I shook it.

"Do you know where you're sitting?" Gloria asked.

"Back that way," Elliott said.

Gloria took two place cards off the table and handed them to Elliot. "Quick like a bunny, switch these for yours and come sit with us." Elliot took the cards and went away, though not quite as quickly as a bunny would have.

Gloria looked at Diane Buckman and said, "It's so good to see you!"

"It's good to see you too, Gloria." She seemed a bit wary, though many people were with Gloria. "We saw each other last night—"

"How is Hilly?"

"Oh, you know how girls are these days."

"I do. My Danielle is at Northwestern. You'd think it was another planet as much as I see her. Do you see Hilly often?"

Diane shook her head, clearly uncomfortable. Then to me, she said, "I love Gloria's column. Sometimes it's the highlight of my day."

"Oh, what a charming thing to say. I do my best to bring a little sunshine into people's lives." With a glance to me she added, "And the occasional thunderstorm."

Diane smiled weakly.

"We should sit down," Gloria said. We all did, just as Elliot came back with their place cards. "Thank you Elliot. I was just about to ask, Hilly's skipping college, is that right?"

"She hates school," Elliot said.

"It was a struggle getting her through high school," Diane said.

"You'd think they'd do a better job, given what we paid," her husband added. *He must mean private high school*, I thought. Otherwise he'd be complaining about taxes.

Given what Gloria had told me about their finances, I wondered if that didn't have something to do with their daughter's skipping college.

"Hilly is such a sweet girl though," her mother said. "Not everyone needs to be book smart."

"Is she working?"

Diane shook her head. Then she tried again to change the subject. "We heard Jane Byrne is going to be here… *and* the mayor. Do you think there will be fireworks?"

Just then, another couple sat at the table with us. They were younger and very chic. They looked like the couple whose photo came in the frame when you bought it: perfect and bland at the same time.

"Hello. We're the Whitmores," he said.

"Kyle and Kelly," she added. It gave me the feeling they did this a lot.

The Buckmans introduced themselves. I did too, though I just gave them my first name. "Nick."

They glanced at Gloria, waiting. I don't think she introduced herself often at these things.

"Oh. Gloria Silver. I write 'The Silver Spoon.'"

"Ah," Kelly Whitmore said, as though she'd just been shot.

Kyle stood up, knocking over his chair. "My mother was Eloise Whitmore."

Before anyone could say anything, he'd stormed off leaving his wife to grab their place cards. I stared at Gloria until she said, "I merely implied that his mother was a lesbian. In print."

"Was she?"

"I hope so. Otherwise she killed herself for no reason whatsoever."

This was one of the thunderstorms she'd mentioned. A bad one.

Waiters hovered nearby. Most of the guests had arrived and the ballroom was close to full. No one came to sit with us. It was interesting being with Gloria. People either flocked to her or ran from her. Very few had no reaction at all.

Soup bowls began to land in front of us. Vichyssoise from the look of it. I asked the Buckmans, "How old is your daughter?"

"She just turned twenty," Diane said.

"And she's here in the city?"

"Yes."

"So I guess you talk to her every day."

"Usually."

"Have you talked to her recently?"

"Who are you again?" Elliot wanted to know.

"Nick Nowak. I'm a private investigator."

"Private—hey, what is this?"

"I think your daughter has been…" And then I couldn't say it. I couldn't say, 'I think your daughter has been murdered and chopped up.' Instead, I said, "…spending time with Rita Lindquist. I think your daughter has been with Rita."

Elliot Buckman's face turned red as a fire engine. I thought he might burst. It took a good five minutes for Gloria to get him calmed down.

It was a good thing the soup was served cold. I wanted it, I was hungry, but it seemed the wrong time to begin slurping away. I did manage to drink the better part of another vodka soda I'd ordered.

"Why do you think Hilly is with Rita?" Diane finally asked, holding her husband's hand tightly on the tabletop.

"Someone using your daughter's name sold some stolen coins to a dealer in Edgewater."

"Using her name? So you don't think it was her?"

"It may not have been," I said. The dealer hadn't described the woman calling herself Hillary Buckman, but I'd described her and he hadn't corrected me. He'd known who I was talking about, though it might have been Possum he recognized. There was a slight chance—

No, I knew it was Rita. I wished it wasn't. For their sake.

"Try to stay calm," Gloria said. "We don't know anything for certain yet."

"When was this coin shop thing?" Elliot asked, his voice thick.

"Tuesday," I said.

"Then it had to be Hilly. Rita was killed over the weekend, wasn't she?"

"Mr. Buckman, does your daughter know who Rita is? Does she know about your connection to her?"

"We're not connected to her," he said. "That's an absurd accusation—"

"Elliot," his wife said.

"She knows to stay away from Rita. Or at least we thought she did."

"It's rebellion," Diane said. "Hilly was such a good teenager. But lately, now that she's grown, now she's having a rebellious streak. I wish, I really do wish, she'd done this at thirteen."

"When was the last time you spoke to your daughter?"

"It's been more than a week," Diane said.

"But we know Hilly's fine. She's using her credit card. I've been keeping tabs on it." That was a foolish assumption, particularly when Rita Lindquist was involved.

"He's such a worry wart," Diane said. "Always checking up on her. That's why she doesn't come home, Elliot. She wants her privacy."

I asked, "Do you happen to remember the charges she's been making? It might help you figure out where she is?"

"Well, um, she took a sightseeing tour on the Chicago River."

"Can you imagine?" her mother asked. "She'd never do that kind of thing with us."

"A grocery store, dry cleaners, Marina City Fashion Nails," he continued.

The last stopped me. I remembered that the corpse had recently had a pedicure—and possibly a manicure—making it more likely that it was their daughter. I asked, "Does she know anyone in Marina City?"

"No," Elliot said, simply.

"Well, not that we know of. We don't know everyone she knows," his wife qualified.

Marina City. Now I was even more sure that's where Rita and Possum were staying—or at least where they had been staying since I chased her out of Andrew Happ's. I just had to figure out what to do with the information.

"This is all making me nervous," Diane said. "There's something you're not saying, isn't there?"

"Does Rita think you have something to do with her father's death?" I suggested.

"We didn't though," Elliot said quickly. "We had no idea the kind of people we were involved with. We're really just victims in this whole thing."

I wondered how true that was.

Chapter Fourteen

I'D JUST TAKEN the first bite of my dessert when someone tapped me on the shoulder. I turned around and there was ASA Linda Sanchez. I was nearly alone at the table, the Buckmans having left and Gloria flitting off to do her job. I could have told Sanchez to fuck off, but then I wouldn't find out what it was she wanted. I indicated Gloria's chair and said, "Have a seat."

She sat down and didn't say anything. I wiped my mouth with a napkin and asked, "What is it you want?"

"I'd like to know what an accused murderer is doing at a society function with Chicago's premiere gossip columnist."

"It's a long story."

"In my experience, the longer the story the less likely it is to be true."

I stared at her for a moment. She was very pretty, lush dark hair and velvet brown eyes. I had the feeling she was unused to men saying no to her.

"Rita Lindquist isn't dead."

"I heard your attorney is floating that ridiculous theory." The way she said it though suggested she thought it was anything but ridiculous.

"It seems very important to you that I be convicted of murder, why is that?"

"Because you're a murderer. Do I need more reason than that?"

"There's a dead girl and you don't know who she is. And what's worse, you don't seem to care. You're willing to ignore the evidence and let Rita—an actual criminal and murderer—get away. All so you can put me in prison. How is that doing your job?"

"We know you work for Deanna Hansen."

"But I don't."

"You met with her at her grandfather's funeral. Is that why you killed Rita? Did you do it on Deanna Hansen's orders?"

"I don't work for Deanna. I just said that. And why would she order Rita's death? Do you have proof they even know each other?"

"I'd say you're the proof."

"Two half-truths don't make a truth."

She smiled as though I'd just paid her a compliment. Then she asked, "Why did you turn down our deal? It was very generous."

Owen hadn't mentioned any deal. He was supposed to even if he knew I wouldn't want to take it. That was strange. And it didn't make me happy.

"Why would I plead guilty? I'm innocent."

"He didn't tell you about the deal, did he?"

I kept quiet.

"I'm surprised. It's an excellent deal. We drop all charges and all you'd have to do was wear an itsy-bitsy little wire."

"So you can bring down Deanna Hansen?"

"So we can bring down one of the biggest criminal enterprises in Chicago."

Of course, she was saying this to me with full knowledge that if I said yes I was very likely to be dead by the end of the week. I was about to say no, but suddenly someone on the other side of the ballroom screamed.

I stood up and looked across the vast room. People were running every which way, some toward whatever was happening, some away from it. The crowd would break every so often and I'd get a good look at Elaine Kelso standing next to a table screaming. I started toward her, having to move people out of the way every few feet.

When I got closer I could see that Richard Crisp was on the floor. One of the guests, presumably one with some medical training, was attempting to help him. There was so much blood I couldn't tell where it was coming from. Crisp's eyes were open and already lifeless.

I walked around to the other side of the table and grabbed Elaine by the arm.

"Tell me what happened."

She screamed again.

"It's important. What happened?"

"Who—"

"Just tell me."

Then she began sobbing. I stood there a moment wondering what I should do. Just as I was about to walk away, she said, "Tall."

"Whoever did this was tall. Is that what you mean?"

She nodded. "Waiter," she gulped and then sobbed some more.

"One of the waiters who was tall. Taller than me?"

She nodded again. Then a gentleman in a tux not unlike mine leaned over to us and said, "He just walked over very casually and leaned over the table. I thought he was going to refill Richard's coffee. But then when he stepped away, Richard was bleeding from his neck."

"Did you see where he went?" I asked.

He waved generally in the direction of the doors we'd entered through. I thought of hurrying over there, but I was sure that whoever it had been was already gone. And then I thought, Possum. It was obviously Rita's friend Possum. It had to be.

Did that mean Rita was also there? I wondered if she'd have the nerve to stick around to watch the aftermath. I started walking around the room looking for her. I didn't get very far when Gloria hurried over to me and asked, "What have you heard? What happened?"

"Someone dressed as a waiter walked up behind Richard Crisp and stabbed him in the throat. Then he ran out the front door of the ballroom. I think it was Rita's accomplice."

Gloria paled. "Such nerve."

"She has less and less to lose," I pointed out.

Just then, several uniforms hurried into the ballroom, followed by a couple of EMTs. The uniforms began to secure the scene, a nightmare with so many people around. I was sure at least fifty people had already slipped away. Possible witnesses. Someone was going to have to get a list of every guest and track them down to see if they'd seen anything. After a few moments of milling around, the EMTs left without the body.

Richard Crisp was dead.

————

IT WAS NEARLY two hours before I found myself seated in front of a young CPD officer giving a statement. During that time, someone had sensibly, or perhaps insensibly, opened the bar. I was feeling no pain.

"Can you tell me what you saw?" he asked. His name was Garner. I read that off his name tag, he hadn't bothered to introduce himself.

"I didn't *see* anything. I *heard* a scream."

"And you looked in that direction. What did you see?"

"People. A lot of people." I was done with another drink. I looked around for a waiter, but the police had, rudely, captured their attention.

"And then what?"

"Well, then I walked over that way."

"You did? You walked toward the murder scene?"

"Yes, but in all fairness… I didn't actually know it was a murder scene."

"Then?"

"There was someone trying to help Mr. Crisp. I think he was a doctor. I hope he was a doctor—is he a doctor?"

"How do you know the victim's name?"

I thought about it. *How much should I tell this guy?* If I told him the truth he was going to get very suspicious very fast. Of course, I couldn't *not* tell him.

"I've heard of him. He's well-known."

Oops, that made him suspicious.

"You're at the scene, standing over the body. Then what."

"I tried to get Elaine Kelso to give me a description of the killer."

"And you know her because…"

"She's also well-known."

"Why did you take it upon yourself to ask for a description?"

That was it. I was going to have to tell him the truth. "I'm a private investigator, and I used to be on the job."

He stared at me a moment. "But you're not on the job."

"No."

"Are you here investigating something?"

That was something I didn't care to answer. It was relevant, certainly, and I knew things the CPD didn't know. I doubted convincing them was going to be worth my time.

Luckily, I was saved by a voice behind me saying, "What are you doing here?"

I turned and there was Detective Monroe White. He was a middle-aged black guy with an expanding and shrinking waist-line. At the moment he looked to be on the decline. I should have been expecting him. We were in the 18th District, after all.

"Hello, Detective White," I said.

"Detective," Garner said. "I'm just taking Mr. Nowak's state—"

And that was all he got out before White said to me, "Didn't I hear that you were in County on a murder charge?"

"I made bond."

Garner looked at me like I'd betrayed him by not mentioning this.

"So where were you when this guy was killed?" White asked.

"He was at table number fifteen—"

"I was having a conversation with ASA Sanchez," I said. I might have been a little smug about it, too. It was a relief to have an ironclad alibi for a change.

"You're drunk."

"It's a party. Open bar."

"Garner, go find out whose bright idea it was to keep serving alcohol, and then shut it down."

"Oh, but could you grab me a vodka soda first?"

"No," White said firmly. Garner got up and hurried off. White sat down across from me. "So what do you know about this?"

"You're looking for a guy named Mike 'Possum' Mazur."

"Why?"

"Because he's the one who killed Richard Crisp."

"You saw him?"

"No. Description."

"You got a description from who?"

"Elaine Kelso."

"She remembers the killer as tall."

"Exactly. Possum is tall."

"You know tall is not a description."

"Possum is Rita Lindquist's accomplice. And she has a motive."

White grabbed a passing waiter and said, "We need a cup of coffee here."

"Vodka soda," I said, changing the order.

The waiter blanched and scurried away. I doubted we'd be brought anything. White stared at me with obvious disgust, then asked, "Isn't Rita Lindquist the woman you killed?"

"No. No, I didn't kill her. She's not even dead."

"Then who did you kill?"

"Nobody. I promise." Well, no one this year. Fortunately, I wasn't drunk enough to let that slip.

"Why do you think Rita Lindquist is still alive?"

"Cause coins."

White sighed. I knew I was being frustrating and not telling this the way it should be told, but I couldn't help it. I took another run at it. "Rita was seen selling some rare coins she stole."

"The dealer knew her and recognized her?"

"No."

"There was a security camera?"

"No."

"Then how do you know it was her?"

"Description."

"Another description?'

I nodded.

"Did he describe her in detail?"

"He said she was busty. Oh wait, no, that's wrong. I described Rita and Possum to the coin guy and he said they'd been there."

He shook his head. "You really should consider another line of work. Let's back up a little bit. Why did *Possum*—" The way he said Possum suggested he really didn't believe there was such a person. "Why did Possum kill Richard Crisp?"

"For Rita."

"And why did Rita want Crisp dead?"

"Revenge. Richard Crisp killed Gunner Lindquist."

"Is that supposed to make sense to me?"

"Back in eighty-three, Lindquist was shot in the back of the head and thrown into the Chicago River."

"Before my time." White had not been with the 18th back then. "And how do you know this?"

"My understanding is that it's common knowledge. So I'd say the more important question is why don't you know it? Huh?"

"Tell me again what you're doing here. Tonight. At this particular benefit?"

"I came to talk to the Buckmans. You see, it's their daughter in the box."

"Why did you kill their daughter?"

It was so annoying when the police did that. Stating the

things you're accused of as though they're facts, hoping you'd screw up and just answer. Drunk. Since I was drunk, I had to be careful about that.

"Noooo, I didn't kill anybody's daughter. Jesus Christ. Possum killed Hillary Buckman. Not me."

"And that's what you came to tell the Buckmans?"

"Sort of. I mean, I wanted to find out some stuff too. In case I was wrong."

"But you're not wrong?"

"Noooo, I'm *not* wrong."

Surprisingly, the waiter came back with a cup of coffee for me. I almost turned it down, but the waiter stood behind White winking. I took a sip of coffee. It was full of whiskey. I watched the winking waiter walk away.

"What does ASA Sanchez have to say about all this?"

"I don't know. We talked about something else."

"And what was that?"

I rolled my eyes. "She offered me a deal. Not a very good one."

"Tell me about it."

I leaned forward and quietly said, "She wants me to help her get Deanna Hansen."

"And she'll drop a murder charge? That sounds like a pretty sweet deal."

"I don't want to end up in the Chicago river. Do you want me to end up in the Chicago river?"

He shrugged like it was no big deal. I realized then, through my fog, that I was making a mistake talking to him. So I said, "I think I want my lawyer."

Chapter Fifteen

THE NEXT MORNING I woke up naked and puking into a bathroom sink. One that I didn't recognize. I ran the water and stood up. Catching a glimpse of myself, I almost puked again. I looked bad: ghostly pale, dark depressions under my bloodshot eyes. I rinsed out the sink and then my mouth. I rubbed cold water on my face. *Where was I?*

I opened the bathroom door and saw I was in a small studio apartment. It had one big window that looked out onto a wall, a portable TV on a bookcase, a café table, and a double bed in a metal frame shoved up against the window with a very naked, very young man in it. He looked familiar, but I couldn't place him.

He saw me standing in the bathroom door and smirked.

"Who are you?" I asked.

He giggled. "Oh my. You were a lot drunker than I thought."

"You didn't answer the question. Who are you?"

"Steven. Or Fitz. My friends called me Fitz."

"How did we meet?"

"I worked the cancer dinner last night. I kept bringing you drinks. You kept trying to tip me."

I squinted at him, mentally putting clothes back on him. I

had a dim memory of him. "You brought me coffee and whiskey."

"I did."

I remembered the Buckmans excusing themselves and Gloria being annoyed because they left before writing a check.

"I'm going to have to make that up to Helena," she'd said.

I also remembered finally starting my soup, only to have it whisked away after a spoonful and a salad replacing it. There was a chicken entrée with a sauce that had chilled to room temperature by the time it reached me. Oh, and a mealy crème brûlée for dessert.

Then I remembered Richard Crisp's murder. I remembered Garner and Monroe White and Sanchez. And I remembered that my life was a total disaster.

"So, did you wanna fuck or what?" Fitz asked.

"Didn't we already do that?"

"Sadly, no. You passed out as soon as I got your clothes off." He squinted at me curiously. "I don't have my contacts in. How old are you?"

"Thirty-seven."

"Oh. You looked a lot younger last night."

"Am I supposed to say thank you?"

"I guess it's just as well we didn't have sex. My friends and I have a pact. No sex with anyone over thirty."

"A pact? Really?"

"AIDS. It's safer to have sex with younger guys."

"It's safer to have sex with condoms."

"Oh God, you're one of those."

"I need to go," I said, looking around the room for my clothes. I noticed a pile of black cloth at the bottom of the bed. Then I remembered I'd spent the night before in a tuxedo. Shit, apparently, I'd be spending the morning in a tuxedo as well.

Picking up the pile, I began to separate it. I found my underwear and pulled them on. Then, I shook out the pants and got a good look at them.

"What's this on my pants? It's sticky."

"Whipped cream. You don't remember?"

"I thought you said we didn't—"

"We played. It was really sexy." Then he said. "You look good in a tuxedo. You look good out of a tuxedo."

"I'm too old, remember. And you promised."

"I'm not very good at keeping promises."

I took a long look at him. He looked really good naked, wrapped in clean white sheets, sunlight coming through the window. It would be so easy to stay for an extra half an hour, to pretend I might not end up back in jail soon, that I might not go to prison, that there wasn't a dead girl in a box. I could make it all go away for a few minutes.

But then I heard myself saying, "I got arrested for murder a few days ago. They might revoke my bond. I have a few things to take care of."

I don't think he heard too much more than "I got arrested for murder..." because he paled and said, "Uh-huh. Um, sure. I get it." Then he asked, "Did you have something to do with that guy who got stabbed last night?"

I shook my head.

"Oh. Okay. Cool."

It took a long, uncomfortable minute or two to put on the shirt and jacket—somehow I'd lost a couple studs. When I was done, I wore a half-open shirt and held a cummerbund but no tie in my hand.

"Have you seen the tie?" I asked.

Stevie shrugged. I was going to have to pay for the tie—and the missing studs. The tie probably came in a set with the cummerbund so I dropped it on the bed.

"Something to remember me by."

"Oh, I won't forget you."

———

WHEN I LEFT Fitz's apartment, I found myself on Brompton across from the Salvation Army Training Center. I decided that was *not* an omen and no one was trying to give me a hint. I walked east to Broadway and then down to the Melrose. I got a table, let the waitress serve me coffee, and then walked back to the payphone between the restrooms.

The restaurant was half-full. Not a single person seemed at all surprised by a thirty-seven-year-old man stumbling around in a dirty tux on a Sunday morning. Welcome to Boystown.

I called Owen Lovejoy, Esquire, at home.

"Why aren't you answering your beeper?" he asked after I said hello.

"I left it at my tailor. It didn't go with my ensemble."

"Don't do that again. I talked to Tony Stork late yesterday. He's desperate to put you in prison. I couldn't budge him an inch. You know what that means, don't you?"

"I'm a lousy lay."

"Someone a lot scarier than me is pulling his strings."

"Yeah," I said. "Linda Sanchez."

"What? How do you know that?"

"She told me."

I let that sit. The line crackled. Finally, I asked. "Why didn't you tell me about the deal they were offering?"

"Because it was ridiculous and I knew you wouldn't take it."

"I wouldn't have. But you should have told me."

"Why?"

"It means something."

"Of course it does. It means they have no case. They're scrambling; trying to get something out of this for themselves. When they realize there's nothing to get, they'll drop it. Where did you see Linda Sanchez?"

"At a benefit dinner. It wouldn't be in the newspaper yet, but Richard Crisp was murdered during the dessert course."

"Who is Richard Crisp?"

"He was on the board at 618 North Wells. And he killed Rita's father."

"Are they going to try and pin that on you?"

"I was sitting with Sanchez at the time."

"Convenient."

"Look, I have a plan."

"Do you?"

It was actually the main reason I'd called—other than making him squirm about the offer from Sanchez.

"This is what I need you to do: Get Tony down to Marina City. ASAP. Unit 3535. I'll wait for you in the lobby. Also, Hamish Gardner and Monroe White."

"How am I supposed to accomplish this?"

"I don't know. Tell them I'll confess if they show up."

"What are they really there for?"

"Rita Lindquist and her friend Possum. I think that's where they've been staying."

"You *think*? Do you have a plan if you're wrong?"

"No."

He stayed silent for a moment. I could feel him calculating the risk. I thought he might try to talk me out of it, but then he kind of owed me for not telling me about the Sanchez offer.

Finally, he said, "I'll see you there in about an hour. Elevenish."

After I hung up, I went back to my table, waved the waitress down, and ordered their hungry lumberjack breakfast. I toyed with the idea of going back to Brian's after breakfast, taking a shower and changing my clothes, but decided against it. Things were going to turn out the way they were going to turn out. What I looked like wasn't going to make a difference one way or another. Plus, I didn't want to be late. It was my show after all.

My breakfast came and I ate every last bite. I tried not to think about anything. My hangover helped in that regard. With any luck we'd be surprising Rita and her friend in their hideout and this whole nightmare would be over.

And then what? What would happen when this was all over? What would I do? Would I just go back to my empty apartment? Did I want to be there without Joseph? Without Ross? I drank half a cup of coffee. A wave of nausea rolled over me, and I wondered if I was going to have to run into the men's room and deposit my eight dollar and ninety-nine cent breakfast into the toilet. But then it passed and I decided I'd better get moving.

I didn't have a lot of cash in my pocket and I had just

enough time, so I walked over to the El, paid my fare, and climbed up to the platform. Once, a long time ago, I'd fallen from the walking bridge that joined the two platforms. I'd landed on an El car and broken my leg. As I waited for the Ravenswood, I looked at the little blue bridge. What would it be like to live someplace that didn't have such fond remembrances? What would a clean slate be like?

A few minutes later, the train came and I got on. It was Sunday morning. There were lots of seats. As we pulled away from the station, I started thinking about a movie my friends had all seen but I hadn't. They talked about it at one of our movie nights, when Brian and Franklin would come over with lots of snacks and we'd watch a video or two. It was a movie where the characters had sex on the El. They thought it was ridiculous that anyone found a car empty enough to have sex in no matter what time of day. I had to admit, I did too.

That started a conversation about the strangest places we'd ever had sex. I think Franklin started it by saying, "I've never had sex on the El, but I did once have sex on an Amtrak train. In the bathroom. This guy from Oklahoma—"

"The *Daily Herald*," Ross said.

"Really?" Franklin said. "An office is the most unusual place you've ever had sex?"

"It's more the particular office." And then he named the well-known publisher of the newspaper. With Earl, they snuck in late one evening.

"Oh, well yes, I suppose," Franklin sputtered.

I'd had sex in an office. Many in fact, but none that important. And alleys, and parks and a limo once. None of it seemed very remarkable to me.

"Mile high club," Brian admitted. Which made me wonder why we thought it so silly to have sex on an El car when it was practically a tradition for people to have sex on an airplane.

"Movie theater," Joseph said, glancing at me. One time I'd thrown a coat over his lap and played around with him.

I don't remember if the conversation worked its way around

to me or what I said, if anything. I did know I was going to miss those movie nights. I was going to miss them a lot.

When we got to the Merchandise Mart, I got off and walked the three blocks to Marina City. Entering the lobby, I immediately saw that I would be dealing with a different doorman. This one was young, barely finished with acne, and looked like he might grow out of his uniform in another week or so. I walked up to the desk, and said, "Can you get the building manager?"

"What do you need? Maybe I can help you."

"I need the building manager."

"You don't live here."

"No, I don't."

"Do you want a real estate agent?"

"No. I think I've just said what I want."

He looked down at the desk in front of him and picked up a business card. He held it out to me. "The building is managed by McEnroe Davis. They're open Monday through Friday, nine to five."

"I need someone who can open up an apartment now. Someone in the building."

"Why do you want to get into an apartment? You don't live here."

I sighed. "Winslow Porter is in Europe. I think someone has been using his apartment."

"Yeah, his niece." He smiled at me in a way that suggested Rita was just his type.

"That's not his niece. The police are on the way. Don't even think about tipping her off. Get me someone who can open a door. And get them now."

He frowned, but said, "Mr. Elber. He's the president of the association."

"Get him."

Reluctantly, he picked up the desk phone and dialed. After a moment he said, "Mr. Elber. This is Keith. The doorman. I have a man down here who... um, it's a situation. Can you come down? Thank you."

He hung up. Looking up at me, he said, "She had a letter and everything. It was on Mr. Porter's personal stationary."

"You're familiar with Mr. Porter's stationary?"

"Well, no… I mean, he doesn't write me letters." As he said that I could see it dawning on him that it's not exactly hard to get stationary printed. With a little skill you could even do it on a Xerox machine.

"Oh."

Just then, Owen Lovejoy, Esquire, walked in. He took in the trashed tuxedo I was wearing, and said, "I'm sure there's a story behind that."

"Some other time," I replied. "Are they coming?"

"Yes, but they're not happy about it," he said.

"Did you tell them I'm going to confess?"

"I tried it with Tony Stork, but he didn't buy it."

"He knows I didn't kill anyone, so he knows I wouldn't confess. How did you convince him to come?"

He just smiled at me. Blackmail. I wondered how many times that would work.

"What about the other two?" I asked.

"I only had to tell them the ASA was coming."

"Oh, by the way, this guy's a witness," I said, indicating Keith, the doorman.

"No, I'm not. I haven't seen anything."

"What did Mr. Porter's niece look like?"

"Black hair, cut really short. Pretty eyes. Really big, um, chest."

"When was the last time you saw her?"

"Couple days ago."

"And the guy who's with her?"

"How did you know—"

"Looks like a possum?"

"I don't know what a possum looks like. I'm from Chicago."

"We have possums," I said. Or at least we did in Bridgeport. I'd never seen one in Boystown.

"We do?"

"Yes. They look like giant rats."

"Oh. I thought that *was* a giant rat."

"What's your name?" Owen interrupted. He'd taken out a pen and one of his own business cards.

"Keith."

"Do you have a last name Keith?"

Reluctantly, he said, "Jasper."

"What's your phone number?"

"Do I have to?" In a matter of minutes he'd gone from sticking his nose in where it didn't belong to not wanting to be involved.

"Yes," Owen said, "You do have to."

Frowning, Keith gave his phone number. "Don't tell my mother what it's about."

"Oh, I never tattle, darling," Owen said, queening it up enough to make Keith go pale.

Monroe White came through the door. He wore the same suit he'd worn the night before. "What is this? I have another hour of paperwork on the Crisp murder and then I can finally go home. You'd better not be wasting my time."

"You won't be sorry."

"I already am."

A small man with graying hair and a little paunch came through the metal security door that led to the apartments.

"Now, Keith, what is this about? I don't understand—"

"Mr. Elber—" I said but got interrupted.

"Detective Monroe White, District 18, homicide." He held out his hand but was ignored.

"Homicide?" Elber nearly squealed. "Oh my God, what's happened?"

"I believe someone's been staying in unit 3535 under false pretenses," I said.

"That's trespassing. He said homicide."

"I'm Owen Lovejoy, Esquire," my attorney said, holding out his card. "Cooke, Babcock and Lackerby."

Elber's head was spinning. "I don't understand what's happening."

"I'm Nick Nowak. I'm a private investigator. I believe a

woman named Rita Lindquist has been staying in Mr. Porter's apartment, along with a man named Possum."

"Michael Mazur," White added. "Ring any bells?"

"This isn't making any sense," Elber said.

And then Hamish Gardner and Tony Stork walked in one after the other. We were a full crew.

"What the fuck is this all about?" Gardner asked. Tony asked a similar question, sans profanity. I tried explaining again, but that didn't go well.

"This is absurd," Tony said. "I'm leaving."

"Well, if he's leaving," Gardner said. "So am I."

"This is nothing but an attempt to muddy the water," Tony whined. "You're trying to get away with murder."

White said, "Let's go upstairs and make sure that's true." He at least knew it might solve an active murder investigation. Two actually.

Tony looked uncomfortable. Of course he did. I now knew Sanchez was pressuring him to get something out of this for them.

"Do you have a search warrant?" Elber asked.

"Jesus Christ," my lawyer said

"We don't need one," I said. "You're going to let us in."

"Don't take legal advice from him," Tony said. "He has no legal background."

"So, I can't just let you in?" Elber asked. "You do need a search warrant?"

"Well, no," Tony admitted. "If you have the authority to let us in…"

"Mr. Porter is in Europe," I pointed out. "We've just told you there might be someone in his apartment. Don't you have a duty to check?"

"Do I?" There was fear in Elber's eyes. I was right, of course. He did have that duty. Then he asked, "But what if there *is* someone in the apartment?"

"There isn't," Tony said. "All you'd be doing is invading a man's privacy—"

"We're right here, Mr. Elber," White said, "with you. You'll be fine."

None of that made Elber any more comfortable. Using a key from a well-stocked key ring, he reopened the metal gate behind him. He held it wide so we could all walk through.

Once the six of us were in the elevator, Owen said to Tony, "The doorman is a witness. He's seen Rita Lindquist."

"He's seen a dead woman?" Tony asked snidely.

Owen pressed thirty-five and the doors closed.

"The description matches," I said.

"What description did he give?"

"Short dark hair—it makes sense that she's dyed it—pretty eyes, big tits."

"That's it? You know she's not the only woman in Chicago with a big bosom." The word bosom sounded funny coming out of Tony's mouth. Like he was trying it out to use in front of a jury someday.

"She was seen with a guy named Mike Mazur, AKA Possum." I said. "He's a friend of Bill Appleton's. He made a withdrawal from Mr. Porter's account with Peterson-Palmer."

Tony's face had turned sour. This was a bit more concrete.

"If you're so smart, who the fuck is the girl in the box?" Gardner eloquently asked.

"A girl named Hillary Buckman. Her parents were involved in 618 North Wells and may have had something to do with Gunner Lindquist's death."

"You have all the fucking answers, don't you," Gardner said, as though it was a bad thing.

"I don't enjoy being accused of murder," I said, just as the elevator doors opened. "But it does tend to make me curious."

Not surprisingly, the hallways in Marina City were round. We curved our way around until we found unit 3535. The six of us stood in front of the door. Nothing happened for a moment.

"I told my wife I didn't want to be on the board. I told her," Elber said, nearly whimpering.

"Why don't we start by knocking on the door?" I suggested.

Elber looked back at the door like he wanted to run from it. I leaned over him and knocked. We waited. Nothing happened.

"See, there's no one here," Elber said. "I guess you all came out for nothing."

"Could you unlock the door?" I said.

"You know, I'm thinking I should call the building's law—"

"Just unlock the fucking door," White growled.

Reluctantly, Elber unlocked the door and opened it a crack. "Hello?"

Elber took a deep breath and stepped into the apartment.

"Check the refrigerator," I told him.

"What?"

"If someone's staying here there will be fresh food in the fridge," I explained. The week before, when Rita had been staying at Andrew Rapp's, there had been a homemade cake in the fridge. If she was here there would likely be food.

Hamish Gardner elbowed by me and went in after Elber. The door was open enough that I could see down a hallway into the living room. A thick metal door led to the half-circle balcony.

Suddenly, Elber turned and pushed past Gardner. He was back in the hallway in a flash. "Someone's been in there. You can tell. It's messy. Mr. Porter would never have left it like that."

"Do we have your permission to enter the apartment?" White asked.

Elber nodded. The rest of us, except Elber, hurried in. On my right, I caught a glimpse of a bathroom and a hallway that led to the bedroom. On my left was the kitchen. It was pink. Entirely pink. The stove was pink, the refrigerator was pink, the cabinets were pink. It made me wonder if Barbie had designed the place.

I went over to the refrigerator and opened it. As I'd expected there was food inside. Recent food. Chinese takeout, half a pizza, a carton of milk and luncheon meat from a deli. At Rapp's, Rita had felt comfortable enough to bake. Here, she didn't want to boil an egg.

I didn't think the kitchen would provide much more information, so I followed the others into the main room. It was set up as half living room, half dining room. Winslow Porter's tastes ran to nineteenth century bordello. There was a red sofa with tufts and carved legs, a large gilt mirror on the wall, and a dining room table that might have belonged to some minor French courtier. All of it ran counter to the ultra-mod style of the building.

"Oh shit," White said from the other room. It wasn't until then that I realized he wasn't with us. "We need to get the Crime Lab out here. There might be blood in the shower."

Gardner and I went through the bedroom into the bathroom. Tony and Owen hung back. The two detectives and I crammed into the small space. The baby-blue bathtub was surrounded by one-inch tiles in various hues of blue. White was pointing out some brownish stains on the grout between the tiles.

"If this is a murder scene then it wasn't cleaned up very well. There are brown stains everywhere," White said.

"Maybe it's not blood. Maybe it's something else. Tea maybe," Gardner said. White gave him a questioning quizzical look.

I was now about four feet away and I couldn't see what they were talking about. It was okay though. I'd take White's word for it. It was entirely possible we were looking at the place where Hillary's hands and head had been cut off. And I didn't need to know that.

The thought of it was more than I could take at that particular moment and I backed out of the room. It's not like I'd never been at a murder scene before. I'd even been at some really gross murder scenes. It was that this murder was so cold, so calculated. Of course, I didn't really know what had happened, what had been planned and what hadn't been. But it didn't matter, a young woman had been killed. And then her body had been mutilated to get revenge on her parents or on me or both. That it was Hillary Buckman was incidental. She wasn't as important as the people Rita could hurt with her plot.

Feeling a bit sick, I went and stood by the floor to ceiling window in the bedroom. I was counting on the skyline views to make things better. I loved Chicago's architecture. It always made things better. The window looked out at the balcony—a quarter pie. There was a thick door that opened onto it, just like in the living room. The bedroom had a peek-a-boo view of the Sears Tower through a couple of buildings. Somewhere down below was the river; I couldn't see it over the edge of the balcony. To the east was the lake, south of us the Loop, and to the west—

I craned my neck to take in the westerly view and found myself looking right into Mike 'Possum' Mazur's face. He'd pressed himself on the other side of the metal door. I have to be honest, he did look like a possum. Beady-eyed and feral.

"Guys—you need to—"

Before I could finish, Possum had opened the door and was running across the bedroom. I ran after him. I got a hand on his shoulder, trying to stop him, or at least slow him down. And it worked—sort of. He came to a stop and slammed me up against a wall. When I hit, it compressed my shoulder over the injury I'd been struggling with since Christmas and I let out a thick oof as pain shot through me like a lightning storm. I fell to the floor.

Gardner came out of the bathroom in time to be shoved aside by Possum and without asking any questions immediately ran after him, yelling, "Stop, Police," as though anyone ever paid attention to that. I could have gotten up and run after them, but the pain in my shoulder was making me dizzy.

Maybe it was time for someone else to break their neck.

Chapter Sixteen

IT WAS OVER.

Well, it was and it wasn't. My lawyer and I spent the next few hours hanging around the laundry room on the twentieth floor. Since Porter's apartment was now a crime scene, Detective White had commandeered the laundry room and turned it into a command post. He wanted statements from us. And, I assumed, wanted to make sure I'd told him everything that was going on. Not that I even knew, I just knew more than anyone else.

Elber was sent to find legal pads so we could write our statements out by hand. White would have them typed and we'd go into the station to sign them.

Possum got away. Not surprising. Hamish Gardner was better at cursing than chasing. But that didn't stop him from wanting in on everything. Didn't happen, though. I heard this exchange with White before he disappeared:

"The guy you just let get away is a suspect in a murder committed last night.

"Yeah, well… this scene is connected to a fucking murder investigation in my goddamn district."

"The only reason you think that is because Nowak told you —a man you've accused of murder which makes him unreliable.

Based on information coming solely from you there is *no* connection. So fuck off."

The look on Gardner's face was priceless. It was like no one had ever sworn back at him—no less a black guy.

Tony Stork hung around the laundry room with us for a little while. He kept his distance, mostly looking out the window, but occasionally sneaking a glare our way. Finally, Owen walked over to him and said, "I want all charges against my client dropped. Immediately."

"No."

"You can't connect him to the murder scene."

"He led us to the murder scene."

"Nick, have you ever been in this building before?"

"Once. Couple days ago I was in the lobby."

"Can you explain how you became aware of unit 3535?"

"There was a withdrawal from Winslow Porter's account a few blocks from here. He's in Europe, so it wasn't him."

He turned back to Tony, "You're going to have to put my client in that unit at the time of the murder."

"I can put your client at the scene of last night's murder."

"He was with ASA Sanchez when that happened."

"That was convenient."

"Hey," I said. "She approached me."

Tony ignored me, and said to Owen, "I'm sure once we get his accomplice in custody we'll have everything we need to put your client away forever."

Then I lost it. "Once I prove the girl in the box isn't Rita Lindquist you're toast. You'll have no motive and I have the perfect defense. Rita and Possum did it. They did it to frame me. And all you've done right from the start is ignore a poor girl's murder."

Ignoring me, Tony spoke to my attorney. "It's him. It has to be him."

"It has to be me because your boss wants it to be me, right?"

"I'm not going to stand here while you accuse—" he abruptly stopped talking and left.

"Well, that was delightful," Owen said.

"Sorry. I should have kept my mouth shut."

"Just relax. We're due in court tomorrow about your bond. I'll argue for the charges being dropped. At this point, all they really have is the jailhouse confession and that won't hold up."

"So this will be over."

"Soon, darling. I promise."

White came down a bit later. He suggested we sit at a table normally used for folding clothes.

"You need to put a uniform by the elevator and a plain-clothes officer in the lobby," I said as we were sitting.

"Yeah? Why is that?" he asked.

"Because Rita wasn't there."

"Where was she?"

I think he was beginning to tire of me having so many answers. "I don't know. Maybe she's out running errands or shopping or at the movies. She's probably going to be back soon and if she sees what's going on before you see her she'll be on the run again."

White looked at me a long moment and said, "I've already posted someone at the elevator *and* in the lobby. So you think this is where the Buckman girl was killed?"

"I do. Don't you?"

"You were kind of drunk last night. So I want to go over this again. Rita Lindquist wants revenge against you because…"

"I ruined her life."

"Why doesn't she just kill you? Murder doesn't seem to faze her. She can't really think we'll never figure out she's not in the box."

"I don't know what she's thinking to be honest. But I doubt she has a high opinion of the CPD. She probably *does* think you'll never figure it out."

"I hope you appreciate how helpful my client is being," Owen said, inserting himself. White kind of glared at me.

"Is Gardner going to be able to connect you to Mazur?"

"The first time I ever saw him was when I found him standing on the balcony."

"And if they were accomplices," Owen pointed out. "Nick

would never have brought you all there. That idea is just absurd."

White raised an acknowledging eyebrow. "You're not a very popular guy, are you Nowak?"

"I've managed to make a few enemies," I admitted.

"I'd say more than a few."

In fact, up until that moment I'd have included White among my enemies. After a thoughtful moment, he said, "I talked to the crime lab guys before I came down. They confirmed that the brown stains in the shower are blood. A lot of it. Mostly down low near the tub."

That was consistent with the idea she might have been dismembered there. He didn't say that outright, though.

"Are you going to take over Gardner's case?" I asked.

"If I can prove the murders are connected," he said. Then after just a moment he said, "Yes."

I wondered how he'd do it, though. My grasp of science wasn't all that strong. I was pretty sure they could type a blood-stain and match it to the blood type of the corpse. There might even have been some other things about the blood that would help. Antigens or pathogens or whatever.

"Do you think we could leave now?" Owen asked.

White thought for a moment. "Yeah, just… when you come by to sign your statements make sure to stop by my desk. I might have a question or two."

"Will do," I said. And then we left.

In the elevator, Owen said, "That went well. This should be all wrapped up by Monday afternoon."

"Can you get the bond back?" I asked.

"Pardon?"

"For whoever paid it. Can you get it back?"

He shook his head. "Doesn't work that way."

"That doesn't seem right. I'm not guilty of anything."

"Bond doesn't have to do with guilt or innocence. It really just has to do with getting out of jail."

"A hundred thousand dollars though. That seems punitive."

"More so when you add my fee," he said with a smile. "Just be glad you don't have to pay it."

"I might be glad, if I knew who put up the money."

He just smiled and kept his mouth very shut.

———

"OH MY GOD, THAT'S FABULOUS!" Brian said when I finally got back to his place. "We need to celebrate."

"I should go see Ross," I said, guilt rushing through me. Why hadn't I been already? Why hadn't I found even a few minutes to go see him?

"Absolutely," Brian said. "He'll want to know you're okay. We should have some champagne first though. Franklin! There's some champagne in the fridge, isn't there?"

"No. There isn't," he called out from the bedroom. "Remember, we drank it when they announced Reagan's cancer."

"Seriously?" I mean, I hated Ronald Reagan, but I wouldn't toast anyone's cancer.

Brian shrugged. "The laugh's on us. He's going to be fine. I'll run over to Treasure Island and get some bubbly." Then he called out down the hallway. "I'm going to Treasure Island."

"Get some pop! Old Coke! I can't stand New Coke!"

"Okay!"

After he left, I went and took a shower. I didn't want to think about how disgusting I smelled; alcohol, vomit, stale cigarette smoke from the party, anxiety perspiration from trying to keep myself out of prison. Peeling off the stinking tuxedo I wondered why Brian hadn't run the minute I came in the door.

The shower, hot and hard, felt wonderful. I tried to clear my mind—everything would be fine, I was going to be okay, my life would go on.

For some reason though my thoughts drifted back to Reagan's cancer. Honestly, I couldn't blame Brian and Franklin for celebrating. His own press secretary had been caught on tape laughing about AIDS—and wasn't fired for it. Not to mention the religious leaders who supported Reagan calling AIDS 'God's punishment.'

Growing up Catholic, I was pretty used to that kind of double-gated logic. If someone Christians approved of died—no matter how painfully—that person was called home to God. Everyone else, though, they were being punished for their sins. It didn't make sense. But if you pointed that out you were told to just have faith. Which I suppose really meant shut up and don't think about it.

Of course, Joseph would point out that God didn't really have anything to do with the craziness people applied to him. It was his belief that we should have faith that God didn't have anything to do with those prickly contradictions. That God made sense even when Christians did not. I had a little trouble with that, too.

I turned the shower off and got out. My heart hurt just thinking about Joseph. I wondered if he didn't think he was being punished now—he was certainly acting that way—if he thought he'd been given a sign, an indication that he was on the wrong path. It was human nature to retreat into religion when things got bad. Was that what he was doing? Or was it that this other guy, Alejandro, needed him more than I did? I had no idea.

I wondered if I should try and find out. Now that I wasn't going to spend the rest of my life in prison, should I chase Joseph down and make him give me answers? If I didn't like the answers, would I accept them?

Scooping up the disgusting tuxedo, I went into the guest room and got dressed in a pair of jeans and a T-Shirt that had a collection of cartoon fish on skateboards. An absurd idea; one that Brian had thought funny enough to buy the shirt for Franklin. Franklin didn't think it was that funny.

I clipped my beeper onto my belt—I hadn't actually left it at the tailor like I'd told Owen. I'd left it in Brian's guest room, which was nowhere near as interesting.

I wondered if there was any point in having the tuxedo cleaned. I wasn't sure it was salvageable. It certainly could never be sold as new. I was going to have to pay for it. That was a bummer. I didn't need or want a seriously used tuxedo.

When I walked into the living room, Terry was sitting on the couch—his eyes and nose red, face swollen, a garbage bag full of clothes sitting next to him. He sniffed.

"Scott broke up with me."

"Okay."

"Fuck you."

'Okay' must have sounded a lot like 'I told you so.'

"What happened?"

"He called me a slut."

"Why did he do that?"

"Because I am one."

"I don't think that's true."

"What do you know? You're a slut too."

"Is there a reason this is important to Scott?"

Terry was quiet. He shrugged a shoulder. "I kind of told him I was a virgin."

It seemed odd to me that it had taken Scott this long to figure out Terry wasn't a virgin. Then Terry explained it. "He was going slow, trying to work me into things. You know, cause I didn't have much experience. I lost my patience and, you know, he figured it out."

"Is he mad because you're not a virgin? Or is he mad because you lied to him?"

"What difference does that make?" Terry asked, looking slightly appalled. Fitz, my not exactly one-night stand came to mind. He and his friends not having sex with anyone over thirty to avoid AIDS. It didn't work, but this was how people were now making decisions. Maybe that's why it mattered to Scott.

I was at a loss. I didn't know what to say to the kid. This is what life was like, things didn't turn out the way you hoped. People you thought were great turned out not to be so great. And that didn't happen just once. It happened all the time. Over and over.

No, that was the last thing he needed to hear. He needed to hear that Scott was a jerk and that the world was full of people who weren't jerks. He'd just been unlucky enough to find one. One of the few. I stood there wishing I could say that, wishing I was a better liar.

Franklin came out of the bedroom and walked into the dining room. "Isn't Brian back?"

"Not yet."

"It's been forty minutes," he said.

"Has it?"

I must have taken a very long shower. Not surprising, I guess, I had really enjoyed it. The Treasure Island was a five-minute walk, so ten minutes back and forth. And he only had to get a few things. He would have been in the store fifteen, twenty minutes tops. Franklin was right, he should have been back already.

"Maybe he ran into someone," I suggested.

"Maybe."

Faced with the prospect of staying there with a depressed Terry and a nervous Franklin, I said, "I'll walk over. Maybe he needs some help with the bags."

"Okay," Franklin said, the beginning of worry on his face.

I went back to the guest room. It was cloudy out and the day was unseasonably cool. Barely even seventy. I threw on my jean jacket and grabbed my keys off the dresser.

"Make sure he remembered the pop," Franklin said as I left the apartment.

On the street, the clouds hung overhead like dingy cotton balls. It was sometime in the afternoon, three, four, I wasn't sure. It had already been a very long day. I was sure I'd find Brian easily. He'd probably just gotten involved with shopping and lost track of time. I walked down Aldine to Broadway.

There seemed to be more people on the street than usual. Men mostly, wearing shorts cut high on the thigh, white high-top Reeboks and expensive T-shirts made with as little material as possible. I could hear music in the distance, "I Will Survive." I remembered there was a street fair on Halsted. I'd gone with Harker a few years back. They closed the street and people walked up and down, listening to music, drinking, eating, buying things.

It felt weird knowing there were hundreds and hundreds of gay guys just a couple blocks away and I was over on Broadway. I felt disconnected, like I'd somehow wandered off and wasn't going in the right direction.

I also didn't see Brian anywhere. Could he have gone over to the street fair? No, that didn't make sense. He wanted to celebrate that I wouldn't be going to prison. If he wanted to go to the street fair he'd have come home and gotten us. He wouldn't have gone alone.

As I walked by The Closet, I noted that the bar was packed to overflowing. I stopped and tried to stick my head in the door. Brian might have seen someone he knew and gone in. But I didn't see any sign of him. After scanning the bar a few times, I continued up Broadway. The street veered slightly to the west and I walked on, passing a transient hotel, a parking garage, the boutiques had stopped and the apartment buildings had begun. I cut across the parking lot when I got to the market. I was beginning to worry.

Inside Treasure Island, I walked the length of the store looking down each aisle as I did. I didn't see him. There were two checkers. One of them wasn't busy. She was somewhere around sixty; gray hair, thick belly, exhausted eyes.

"Did you see a guy come in earlier, twenties, blond, good-looking?"

"Really? In this neighborhood? We get fifty guys who look like that in here every day."

"I think he was wearing a blue shirt. Pink shorts?"

She gave me a disgusted look and said, "That doesn't help."

I made a point of thanking her, though for what I had no clue. I walked outside and stood there. This was ridiculous. There were dozens of things that could have happened, none of them sinister. He could have gotten pulled into The Closet and I just didn't see him. He could be over at Big Nell's. He could be at the street fair. It was really only a block or so away, he might have decided to spend five minutes there and then time got away from him. Or he could have decided to walk out to Lake Shore and take in the view on the way home. There were half a dozen ways I could have missed him.

I walked back down Broadway to Aldine, taking the time to peek into every little business on the way. I was halfway down Aldine when I saw the big, black limousine double parked in front of Brian's building.

And I knew it was there for me.

Chapter Seventeen

THIS HAD HAPPENED BEFORE. A few years back, Jimmy English had shown up outside my apartment on Roscoe and asked me to find out why his grandson—who'd killed his stepfather—was refusing to assist in his own defense. It probably hadn't been hard for Jimmy to find me. I was in the phone book, after all.

I knew Deanna Hansen was in the limo even before the chauffeur got out and came around to open the passenger door. The fact that she'd found me at Brian's condo suggested she was pretty savvy. Or, more likely, that we shared the same attorney.

I climbed in and took a good long look at her. She wore khakis, Keds, a peach-colored Polo shirt and a thin, white cardigan. She looked like a nice young mom from a northern suburb who'd slipped away for a little Sunday shopping. The hardness in her face made a lie of the outfit, though. When I'd first met her she was an undergrad at Loyola. There had been an innocence about her, and a stubbornness too. That was long gone. Well, the innocence. The stubbornness was still there.

"It was you," I said. Certain things suddenly made sense. "You paid my bond."

She smiled. "I'm not hearing a thank-you."

"I can pay you back," I said, boldly. I had about seventy-five thousand from the Harker's condo and Bert's various savings accounts. I was pretty sure Sugar would lend me the other twenty-five.

Deanna laughed, though, and said, "You don't have that much money."

"I can pay you a hundred grand."

"But you owe nearly twice that."

"No, I owe you a hundred."

"I paid your legal fees."

"It's been less a week. They can't be that high," I said. Actually, they could be. I'd taken up most of Owen's attention. And, of course, if Deanna wanted them to be high, they would be.

"And then there's the interest." Which could also be as high as she wanted.

"Then fuck you," I said. "I didn't ask you to post my bond, I didn't ask you to pay my legal fees. We never had an agreement. We have no contract."

She gave me a look like I was being ridiculous—and I probably was. She went on, "We both know we're not on our way to court, so whether or not there was a contract is a moot point. Five years. That's all I'm asking. I'll pay you. I'll pay you well. And in five years the debt will be gone."

"Unless you change the contract," I said.

"It wouldn't be wise for me to do that. I don't want to get a reputation as someone who can't keep her word. That would be bad for business."

"I never did anything illegal for your grandfather. I have a feeling you don't understand that."

"No, I do. I have other people for that kind of thing."

"Then I don't get it. What do you need me for? What is it you think I can do for you?"

"The kind of people I can get to do… what's necessary… aren't very bright. I need someone smart. Someone with principles. To keep everyone in line."

"Including you?"

"No. Not including me." For the first time she bristled. She wasn't going to be the kind of boss who took criticism well, that was obvious.

My future lay before me. There would be money and stability and moral ambiguity. Actually, I'd be lucky if it was only ambiguity. It would more likely be immorality. I might not be expected to hurt people myself, but I'd certainly be expected to assist. To track people down, to bully them, to threaten them. To lead the way to their deaths even. I didn't want to do it. Couldn't do it. I also knew I wasn't getting out of the car unless I said yes.

"All right," I said.

"Really? That was easier than I thought it would be."

"You're not leaving me a lot of options."

She smiled in acknowledgment. "I'd like to buy Dresden."

"The city in Germany?"

"Don't be cute. The bar under the El at Belmont."

I knew exactly what she talking about. Her grandfather had been extorting the bar, or at least he had until the owner filed a complaint with the liquor board. I don't know that much happened with it, other than its being a footnote in the Federal investigation of Jimmy English.

"I didn't know the bar was for sale."

"It's not."

"Generally, it's hard to buy something that's not for sale."

"That's where you come in. I need something on Jonathon Lidell. Something that will make him want to sell to me."

"I think that's called blackmail."

"Your job is to get the information. You have no idea what I do with it." She watched me, waiting to see if I was going to balk.

"Sure, give me a week."

I opened the door to get out of the car but stopped and sat back into my seat. I stared right into her eyes and said, "Linda Sanchez."

"What about her?"

"She wanted me to wear a wire. That's why they tried to railroad me. So I'd make a deal."

She smiled serenely. Too serenely.

"That's not what's been going on, is it?" I had that old sick feeling in my stomach, the one I get every time someone pulls one over on me.

"Tony Stork," she said, then asked me to close the door.

The limo pulled away as I stood on the sidewalk trying to understand what she said. Sanchez wasn't the one pressuring Tony to prosecute me. It was Deanna. Just as her grandfather must have taught her, she worked both angles. She got me out of jail and then made sure I was threatened with a lifetime of confinement. A chill ran up and down my spine. How would I ever get away from her?

―――――

WHEN I GOT UPSTAIRS, I went right for the phone and called Owen Lovejoy, fucking Esquire. Franklin stood in the kitchen door, Terry was collapsed on the couch watching an old Cary Grant movie. I barely noticed them.

Owen picked up. "Hello?"

"Deanna Hansen was here. You sold me into slavery."

"I wouldn't call it slavery, that's being overly dramatic. Indentured servitude perhaps."

"Don't split hairs. You had no right to do that."

"I didn't *say* I had a right to do it. If you asked me, which you haven't, I would say I had no choice."

"What does that mean?"

"Why are you angry, Nick? She offered you a job and I assume you turned her down."

"She's not letting me turn her down."

"And why do you think it's any different for me? Offers that can't be refused. That's her business, she's learned it well."

I began to soften. She had Owen over a barrel, not the same barrel she had me over, but a barrel nonetheless.

"You should have told me. You should have been honest with me."

"Would you rather be on the fast track to Joliet? Prison is rarely the better choice."

"Fuck you."

"Yes, well, fuck you too, darling."

I hung up on him.

What was I going to do? I couldn't work for Deanna. I had to find a way to get away from her. Maybe I could do what she did, maybe I could find something on her that she didn't want —she was a criminal, a very public one, was there anything—

"You didn't find him?" Franklin asked, pulling me back to reality.

"Find who?" Terry asked, not looking up from the TV.

"Brian," I said, then asked Franklin, "How long has he been gone?"

"An hour and a half," Franklin said, his voice cracking. "It's not like him."

"He was going to get champagne. So—what if he didn't like what they have at Treasure Island?"

"He knows what they have there. If he didn't want that he'd have said he was going somewhere else."

"Why did he want champagne?" Terry asked.

"Nick's not going to prison."

Terry rolled his bloodshot eyes like that was ridiculous.

I said, "Maybe Brian changed his mind on the way."

"You think he went to Jewel?" Franklin asked, doubt in his voice. And he was right. Jewel did not have a better selection. Nor did the two or three liquor stores dotting the neighborhood. And they certainly weren't an hour and a half away. Then, he said, "We should call the police."

"No, we shouldn't," I said firmly. "He's been gone less than two hours. They won't do anything."

"But isn't that what they're there for?"

"Yes, but people disappear for short periods of time every day."

"Brian wouldn't."

"I agree with you. The police won't."

"You think something happened to him, don't you?"

"I don't know."

"Hospitals. We should call hospitals."

"Maybe he went to see Ross," Terry suggested.

"I should call the nurse's station," Franklin said. He went looking for the cordless phone which was somehow never on its base.

"We should probably go through his address book. Check to see who else we should call," I said.

"Found it," Franklin said, holding up the phone. He dialed the hospital's number from memory. "Hi, I'm wondering if anyone has seen Brian Peerson around. He'd be visiting Ross Buckley."

I started looking for Brian's address book. I found it in one of the built-in drawers in the china cabinet. The book was from the Art Institute, each page containing a great work of art, mostly French Impressionism, including the really famous one that had been made into a musical.

"Uh-huh. Okay. If you see him tell him to call home. We're worried about him." Franklin hung up. "He's not there."

"Do you know many of his old friends? He used to hang out with a crowd at Big Nell's," I said, holding out the address book.

Franklin took it and stared at it. "No, I don't think he sees any of those people. Not anymore."

"He might have walked over to the street fair and run into one of them."

Franklin shook his head. That didn't sound any more plausible to him than it had to me. "Something bad has happened. I know it."

"Don't assume that. There could be a very logical explanation," I said, but what I felt was dread. Something had happened to Brian and I didn't know what. "He's not sick at all, is he?"

"What do you mean?"

"I mean, he couldn't have passed out, had a seizure, taken a bad fall?"

"I don't think so. I mean, he would have told me. I would have noticed. I'd know."

Then something hit me. "He could have been arrested."

"Do you think so?" Franklin asked. "Why?"

"I don't know. But let's call Town Hall Station."

Chapter Eighteen

JUST AS I was about to dial the phone, my beeper went off. It said: 819. I had no idea what that meant. Was it a wrong number? A misdial? That had never happened before, but I guess it could. Then I realized I had the damn thing upside down. What it really said was 618.

I knew what that meant. The page was from Rita. 618 North Wells. That's where she was. That's where Brian was. That was bad. That was *really* bad. It was something I hadn't let myself think about; but—if I was honest—it had been at the back of my mind from the moment Brian couldn't be found.

Why did she have to take Brian? I would have gone if she'd just sent—no, I wouldn't have. Well, not alone. I'd have gone with the police just like I had that morning. That was easy enough to figure out. She wanted me, needed me, to come alone. And she knew if she had someone I cared about I wouldn't involve the police.

Was she right? Should I call the police anyway? A murderous pair with a hostage was exactly what they were there for. And if I had even the slightest bit of confidence in the CPD, I might have. But I didn't. All I could imagine were a hundred scenarios where everything went wrong and Brian ended up dead. As nearly as I could tell Brian's chances were a whole lot better if I went on my own.

I had to leave. I had to get there. And I couldn't tell Franklin where I was going. Of course, I didn't have a weapon. Thank you, CPD. Given that they'd likely be dropping the charges I could probably have gotten my guns back within the week, but that was no help. There wasn't any time limit on Rita's 'invitation,' but I was sure a week was too long.

I didn't know anyone with a gun. Brian certainly didn't have one. And Franklin, well, no. I went into the kitchen and opened a couple of drawers looking for a knife. There were two big ones, roughly ten inches long and three inches thick. They would do the job, but how exactly could I carry them around? And how did I walk up to Rita with a knife I couldn't hide and get her to give me Brian? Instead, I selected a boning knife and a paring knife. I could manage to hide both in my clothing.

What else did I need? The unfinished building was at least twenty stories. I had no interest in climbing it, but I might have to. All I had were my Reeboks. I wondered if I should go back to my apartment and get an old pair of Nikes, but decided against it. I went into the bedroom and put on the disgusting jacket to the tuxedo, then I put one knife into a side pocket and the other, the longer one, into the inside breast pocket.

I looked up from what I was doing and noticed Franklin standing in the doorway. He asked, "Where are you going?"

"I'm going to look around the bars.'

"I'll go with you."

"No. You need to stay here in case he comes back."

"Terry's here."

I lowered my voice, "Yeah, um, someone reliable."

Franklin took a long moment. I could tell he wanted to contradict me but couldn't. He turned and left the room. I looked around. I had no idea what I was walking into. I'd need more than just two knives. Maybe that was ridiculous, maybe I was being overly cautious, but better safe than sorry.

As I walked through the apartment, I remembered that Brian kept a few of his mother's things on the built-in cabinet in the dining room: a blue-and-white bud vase, a delicate tea cup, a paperweight. I grabbed the paperweight and slipped it into a pocket. It was glass, egg-shaped and about twice the size of a large egg, filed flat on the bottom, and inside had a delicate red flower made of glass then encased in glass. It was heavy and solid, fit nicely in my palm and would crack a skull.

I was nearly out of the apartment when Franklin said, "Nick, he's not in the bars. You know that."

"I have to try," I said and hurried out the door.

I found Harker's old Lincoln over on Roscoe near my old apartment, jumped in, and drove down to Wells and Ontario. It was a quiet neighborhood. Not a lot of residential buildings, plus it was Sunday night. It was roughly an hour before sunset, the sky was steel gray and the light waning.

I pulled over to the curb across the street from the half-finished building on Ontario. It took up one corner of the block. The lot was circled in plywood fencing—now plastered with posters of upcoming rock concerts, most of them for R.E.M.—and a scaffolding built to prevent building materials falling on the heads of pedestrians.

The lot itself was maybe two hundred feet down Ontario and a hundred on Wells. Two sides abutted hundred-year-old brick factories which now housed failing family businesses—a mattress maker, a furrier—or they housed nothing at all.

At the west end of the Ontario side, I noticed a dip in the sidewalk. That had to be some kind of entrance. I also noticed there was a gate made of metal fencing crossing the dip. I crept down the block and parked directly across from the Ontario entrance. The parking spot was illegal, but a ticket was the least of my worries.

I got out of the car and stared up at the unfinished building. The bottom ten floors already had windows and gray granite slabs attached. The floors above lost their windows and eventually the granite, leaving nothing but bare girders with thin concrete and rebar floors strung between them. Way up top was a crane.

I had a bad feeling in my stomach that I was going to have to climb up there. I wondered if Rita was looking down at me right then. I searched the building looking for her, but in the dimming light I couldn't see much.

First, I was going to have to get through the fence. I walked over to the gate and gave it a little shake. The chain holding it together fell loose. Well, that was easy. Too easy. This was probably how Rita and Possum had been getting in and out. And since they'd invited me, they'd made it easy for me to follow them inside.

How much time did they spend here? I wondered. And what did they do when they came? Then I had a funky thought. This must have been the address where Rita had sent Hilly Buckman's body. So, why? Why here? She knew there'd be no one to accept it. She knew it would be returned. She could have just made up any address—although if she'd been wrong and actually sent the body somewhere real…

Had she been deliberately leaving me a clue? If I'd looked closely at the box when it was in the hallway outside my office, I might have known something was wrong. But I hadn't. I'd had no reason to. So was she taunting me? Knowing I'd miss the clue altogether. I couldn't think too much about that, not just then.

Standing there at the entrance, out in the open, all I could think about was the fact that Rita had a gun. She'd shot me with it. I tried to remember what kind it was. A .38 Special, or at least it was in my memory. Those guns weren't too accurate over fifty feet unless you spent a lot of time on a firing range. So, if Rita was in there waiting to shoot me she was probably close—provided she didn't have another weapon altogether which was, unfortunately, possible.

I tried looking sideways through the fence. Not an easy task, it was pretty close to the plywood wall. I knew I would step through the gate sooner or later, so I just went ahead and stepped through. I searched each floor again looking for Rita or Possum. Everything seemed especially still. Disturbingly so.

I can't say I have a lot of experience with construction sites, but I still knew there'd be a temporary elevator somewhere attached to the side of the building. I mean, they couldn't put in the nice elevators until they were finished. So I should find that elevator.

Or stairs. Finding stairs would be better. They'd know where I was if I came up on the elevator. It would make a lot of noise. I needed to find a way into the building and then find the stairs. The entrance was in the front, on the Wells side of the building. There was probably a way in down there.

Instead of rushing down I stayed where I was. In front of me, a ramp led down to the parking garage below the building. The darkness started almost immediately making the entrance look like the entrance to a cave. A scary cave. I wondered if there was an entrance to the building down there. A staircase that went up to the first floor and possibly continued upward. Finished buildings had them.

I can't say I loved the idea of stumbling around in the dim light looking for the stairs. Instead, I decided to go down and look at the front of the building first to see if there was a way—

There was a flash of light in the garage below me. At first I wondered if I'd really seen it. I stood very still, waiting for it again. And then there it was. They were down there, in the garage, underground. Rita, Possum and Brian. I almost started down the ramp but stopped myself.

What were the flashes of light? A flashlight? A match? The light was deliberate. They wanted me to come down the ramp. They were already in the dark, giving them the advantage. At least for the first level I'd have some light behind me. They'd see me, but I wouldn't see them. And…

If Rita had some kind of flashlight she could shine it in my eyes and then her friend could shoot me. That didn't seem like a good way for this to end up. I backed out of the gate and crossed the street to my car. I opened the trunk of the Lincoln. I needed some help.

Harker had an emergency kit. I'd only opened it once, so I didn't know everything in it, but I did have some idea. When I was on patrol we always carried a kit around in the trunk. You get used to that. I reached in and pulled it to the edge of the trunk. I unzipped the black duffle it was in and began poking around.

There was a flashlight. I pulled it out and flipped it on. Nothing happened. I unscrewed it and dumped the D battery out. It was a corroded gooey mess. Not surprising, I suppose. Harker might have last checked the bag when he bought the car, which was somewhere around seven years before. I took a quick look around for some backup batteries but there weren't any. There were, however, two flares. They looked pretty good—or at least better than the battery—I put them in my back pocket. The other things in the bag: jumper cable, gloves, bandages, burn cream—didn't seem like they'd be useful.

I went back through the gate. Standing there at the top of the ramp, I knew that Rita had the advantage. She knew I was coming. She had a gun, she had an accomplice, she had the dark. I needed to figure out how to take those advantages away from her. I considered creeping slowly down the ramp, but she'd be expecting that. So I did the opposite. I ran down the ramp as fast as I could. I needed to get into the dark as quickly as possible. The dark was dangerous, but it was also safe. It put us on a more equal playing field.

In a matter of seconds, I couldn't see where I was going. I turned at the point where I thought the ramp would end and began to descend in the other direction. When I did, I clipped an abutment, stumbled, and ended up on the hard concrete. That was lucky. A gunshot flew over my head.

For the briefest moment, the flash from the gun illuminated Rita holding her .38. Behind her Possum held a bound and gagged Brian. And then we were in the black again. I didn't move. I had no idea whether she'd gotten a glimpse of me or not. When she didn't fire again, I assumed she hadn't.

Waving my hands in the dark, I found the abutment I'd bumped into. It was just to my right. In a quick move, I stood up and slipped behind the piece of concrete. I braced myself for another gunshot, but it didn't come. I reached back and pulled one of the flares out of my back pocket. As quietly as I could, I took the cap off, turned it around and was ready to strike the flare. Taking a deep breath, I struck. The end of the flare lit and I immediately threw it as best I could toward the far wall. It bounced off and began rolling down the ramp.

Rita fired at it.

The flare was halfway down the ramp, returning the top to darkness. I took that opportunity to run across the ramp to the far wall. Following the wall with my hand, I crept down the ramp a good ten or twelve feet toward them.

Unfortunately, Rita and Possum were withdrawing, dragging Brian with them, retreating further into the garage. The flare stopped rolling and settled on the flat landing area between the ramps. Now there was a pool of crackling light between us. Separating us.

A thought popped into my head. *Rita assumed I had a gun.* That made sense. The last time we'd met face to face, I'd had one. She didn't realize the police had taken it away from me. That's why she wasn't advancing, wasn't using her flashlight to find me and shoot me. I had to keep moving quickly so she didn't figure that out.

The wall next to me was solid, but the wall across from me, the one between the ramps, that wall opened up half way down the ramp and became concrete posts and open rebar. I ran across to the inside wall, then took a few steps down to the spot where it began to open.

"Rita," I called out. "Let my friend go. I'm here. That's all you needed him for. He'll just slow you down."

As soon as I'd said the last, I realized I might have made a mistake. There was nowhere for her to go but down. She was trapped. Right? No, there had to be an elevator to take people up to the building—although that probably hadn't been installed yet. Stairs. There had to be emergency stairs. But where? I hadn't seen anything—not that I'd seen much. There must be an entrance on each level, though. There could be one right behind where Rita and Possum were. I had to assume they knew their way around better than I did.

"Fuck you," Rita said in the darkness. "You ruined everything."

"You're just making things worse for yourself." That was such a cop thing to say, I could barely believe I'd said it. "Look, if you let Brian go I'll let you leave. You can get away. Leave Chicago, set up somewhere else."

She answered me with a gunshot. The flash gave me an idea of where they were. They were at the bottom of the ramp next to me. I reached back and got the other flare from my pocket, took the cap off and struck it. Once I had it lit, I threw it through the opening onto the ramp below. It rolled down toward them.

There was another shot. Followed by hurried footsteps as they went down further into the garage. Running down the ramp, I snatched up the first flare and ran down so I could throw it through the rebar onto the ramp below where they would now be.

Another shot. How many was that? Four? Her gun only held five bullets. She could have more with her. She could have a lot more with her. But she'd have to take time to reload and that would be my opportunity.

I listened as they ran further down in the garage. There was a flare just below me on the platform and one on the platform below me that I couldn't see. Rita and Possum and Brian were somewhere below the flares. I wondered how deep the garage was. How long before we ran out of garage completely.

I walked down to the landing below me and picked up the flare. I was about to go down the ramp and drop the flare onto what I assumed was their present location, when I realized something was wrong. There should have been a flare at the bottom of this ramp—but there wasn't.

Slipping down to the opening on the inside wall, the only light I could see was the flare in my hand. The other flare was out. That was wrong though. Flares lasted longer than that, much longer. They must have stomped it out.

I had to do something. I couldn't stand there with a flare in my hand and wait while Rita reloaded her gun. I had to act now while I had a chance. I rushed down the ramp, threw the flare onto the ramp opposite, and kept running.

When I turned to continue downward, I saw that they were at the bottom. Possum was stomping on the second flare, while Rita raised the gun and fired at me. Lucky me, she missed. That was five. Had she already reloaded? No. No, she hadn't. She was taking a purse off her shoulder and crouching down onto the ground to look through—

Then light was gone. Possum had extinguished the flare. I reached into the breast pocket of the tuxedo and pulled out the boning knife. Then I ran down the ramp toward Possum's last position. Either I miscalculated or he moved, because I ran right into him with a thud. With my free hand, I reached up and felt his face. Before I did anything, I had to make sure I hadn't accidentally run into Brian. He was tall and there was no gag. It was Possum.

He got his hands around my throat and began to squeeze. Without even a single thought I stuck the knife into his belly. Then I pushed it deeper. He groaned deeply. In a wet, rasping voice he said, "Rita. Rita kill him."

Stepping back, I pulled the knife out, feeling his blood cover my hand and spill down the front of me. I couldn't think about that, though. I pushed the fact of it out of my head. I could hear Rita rooting around in her purse looking for bullets. I had to stop her before she could reload her gun.

With my free hand, I swung into the dark where I thought she might be. I clipped her face. I don't know whether I pushed her off balance or whether it was simply the surprise of being hit in the face, but I heard her fall with a loud, "Oomph."

I took a guess and kicked into the darkness. Nothing. I tried again, this time connecting with Rita's purse. The contents of which were now scattered across the ramp. Rita let out a frustrated growl and then something hard and metal crashed into my face. She'd hit me with her snub-nosed revolver, possibly breaking my nose. Instinctively, I brought up the knife and swiped it at her. I missed, but not by much. She grabbed my hand, pulled it toward her, and bit down on it. Hard.

I dropped the knife and yelled, "Fuck!" I slammed the heel of my free hand into her face. She grunted but then jumped on me. For a moment it seemed like she was everywhere, biting me, pulling on my hair, trying to stick her fingers into my eyes. With one hand I tried to peel her off me. With the other, bloodied hand, I reached into my jacket pocket and grabbed the paperweight.

Into my ear she whispered, "Die, die, die."

With her clinging to me, I couldn't hit her hard enough with the paperweight to do any real damage—and only real damage would slow her down. I shook her off and then swung as hard as I could. I connected with her head and heard her go down, hard. I kicked where I thought she might be and connected with something. Her hip, maybe. She didn't make a sound. I didn't have time to worry whether she was unconscious or just dead.

"Brian. Where are you?"

He made a muffled noise behind his gag. I followed the sound. I bumped into him, nearly knocking him over. I reached up and felt a shoulder, following that to his neck, then around to the back of his head. The gag was packing tape wrapped around what felt like a sock in his mouth. I pulled at the tape. It was hard to break, but I did loosen it. I was able to pull the sock out of his mouth.

"My hands, get my hands."

I felt around the back of him. His hands were bound with the same tape. I began pulling at it, loosening it as I had the gag. Then I stopped. What was I doing? I had a paring knife in my pocket. I pulled it out and managed to cut the tape off Brian's hands. Then, I reached up to take off the gag, but Brian was already working the tape over his head.

"How do we get out of here?" he asked.

I took him by the hand and began walking toward what I thought was the outer wall. I held my free hand in front of me, moving it from side to side in case I encountered something I wasn't expecting. I was pretty sure there was nothing down here but the parking ramp, but I didn't want to find out the hard way that I was wrong.

I found the wall and let go of Brian's hand. "Grab hold of

my jeans in the back. He felt around my back, reached up under the tux jacket and got hold of my jeans. I took a moment to wipe my bleeding nose. Big mistake. I almost whimpered from the pain.

With one hand touching the wall and the other out in front of me, I led us up the ramp rather quickly. In a short time we were standing at ground level looking down into the parking structure we'd just come out of. Brian said, "You killed two people, didn't you?"

"I don't know. I might have."

I thought the next thing he'd say would be that it was wrong or that we needed to call the police. Instead he asked, "Did you leave any evidence?"

"I left a knife," I said. "With my fingerprints on it."

"Nick, you need to get the knife."

Shit. I had to go back down in there. I should have thought things through. For a moment, I didn't know if I could do it. Then, I told myself not to think. To just do.

"Stay here," I said, and then I began to retrace my steps, back down into the darkness. I moved down quickly, using the same method I'd used coming up. One arm on the wall, one in front of me. I moved quickly because I knew it was unlikely I'd encounter anything.

Chapter Nineteen

FUMBLING AROUND IN THE DARK, I knew I was probably leaving footprints in Possum's blood. Better they have my shoe size than my fingerprints. Still, just to be safe, I deliberately slid my feet around to obscure any prints. I crouched and felt around Possum. I was pretty sure he was dead. I began close to his body and then branched out.

It was quiet, the only sound I heard was my own breathing. Finally, I found the knife and snatched it up. Slipping the knife into the pocket of the tux jacket, I stood fully erect. I knew I should just walk over to the wall and feel my way back up to the surface. But there was something I wanted to check, something I needed to know. *Was Rita really dead?*

I moved my foot around in the dark, trying to find her body on the floor. Nothing. Nothing at all. I stepped on her purse. I stepped on some of the things that had fallen out of it—breaking them with loud crunches. But no Rita. I kept kicking my foot around. I began to get the sick feeling she wasn't there.

She was alive.

Brian. I'd left Brian alone. I hurried over to the wall. Keeping one hand on it, I ran, ran in the pitch black, ran upwards until I was at the top of the ramp.

"Brian. Brian where—"

He stepped out from where he'd been standing next to the

base of the building. "Sorry. I had to pee. I've had to pee for like the last hour."

"I couldn't find Rita. I think she's still alive. I think she's somewhere around. We have to get out of here."

I led Brian over to the open gate and then across the street to my car. We got into the car. Brian dug around in the glove compartment as I pulled away from the curb. He handed me a tiny packet of tissues. I shoved a couple up my nose.

"Are you all right?" I asked.

He ignored that and asked, "What does it mean if Rita's alive?"

"I don't know," I said, honestly.

"She'll come after you again."

"I'll have to figure out how to stop her." And I would have to figure out how to stop Deanna Hansen and ADA Sanchez from coming after me too. For a moment that was overwhelming. I had to hold tight to the steering wheel and focus on the road.

About then, I began to feel sticky. Possum had bled all down the front of me. And then I'd bled all over me. My shirt was glued to my chest with blood.

"What if you can't make her stop?" Brian asked.

I didn't know what to say to that. He was asking if he should be afraid that Rita would come after him again. The adrenaline from saving Brian had worn off and the realization that I'd put my friend, my dear friend, in danger had begun to take hold. And it wasn't just Brian, it was anyone close to me. Anyone close to me was in danger as long as Rita was alive.

It sounded terrible, but I couldn't help wishing I'd done a better job of killing her. I'd thwarted her again. She was going to be very angry. I was going to have to stay away from Brian. And Sugar. And Terry. And anyone else I cared about even a little.

"You need to throw it away," Brian said, when we'd gotten as far as Fullerton.

"What?" I asked.

"You need to throw the knife away. Somewhere they'll never find it."

"Where?"

"Go west," he suggested. "Cut over to a major street like Lincoln or Ashland."

I turned on Diversey and began heading west. "What are we looking for?"

"I don't know. An alley? Apartment building. Someplace with a dumpster."

We drove around. There were a lot of apartment buildings on Diversey, some of them looked big, but I thought it might be better to get out of any neighborhood I was familiar with. Ashland was a street I barely used, so I went straight for it.

At the light, I turned north and drove a few blocks until I saw what I wanted. On my left was a Jewel market. I turned on Wellington and went around to the back. Along the wide, solid brick wall at the back of the store was a metal dumpster. I pulled into the loading area, jumped out of the Lincoln and lifted the lid to the dumpster. I dropped the knife in.

When I got back into the car, I said, "My guess is they empty that pretty often."

Brian nodded. He looked a little pale. I wondered if he might be going into shock. "Are you okay?"

"Yeah. I want Franklin."

I nodded. He was probably in shock. "We'll be home in a few minutes."

Cutting back over to Ashland, I drove up to Belmont then I turned toward the lake. I tried to say a few encouraging things as I drove. "You'll be okay. It's all okay." I think I said them as much for me as I did for Brian.

When we got to Aldine, I pulled around the back of his building and parked in the alley. We went up the wooden staircase on the back of the building up to Brian's backdoor. He unlocked the door and we walked into the kitchen.

Franklin was wiping down the counters. He was kind of a neat freak; I wasn't even sure the counters needed wiping. When he turned around and looked at us the look on his face made me wonder if he might have a stroke right there.

"It's not ours," Brian said quickly. "It's not our blood."

"Okay. Whose is it?"

"Rita's friend," I said. "Accomplice, whatever."

"Is he dead?"

"They kidnapped me. Nick saved me."

"Okay." He looked concerned. "And the police just let you go?"

"We're not calling the police," Brian said. "They won't treat Nick fairly. You know that."

"Yes, but—" Franklin was struggling with this. He was a rule-follower even when the rules were wrong. "It was self-defense, though. If they kidnapped you—"

"We're not calling the police," Brian said, in a tone I very rarely heard from him. Franklin seemed to recognize it right away. Brian was putting his foot down and clearly not for the first time. Though certainly the first time in front of me.

"What about Rita?" Franklin asked.

"She got away," I admitted.

"So this could all happen again?"

"It won't," I promised. "I'll make sure it doesn't."

"How? How are you going to do that?"

"Franklin, this isn't the time. We just—it was awful. I think we just want to forget it."

But Franklin was right. We couldn't just forget it. Rita was likely to regroup and then anyone close—

"I'm going to stay away from you guys," I said.

"What? No. You can't do that."

"I need to get out of these clothes and then I'll get out of your way."

"Nick, stop it," Brian said. "Franklin, tell him he doesn't have to leave."

But Franklin didn't say anything. I walked out of the room and went to take a shower and gather my few belongings. While I was in the shower I could hear them fighting. As I was toweling off, a door slammed and it got quiet.

In the bedroom, I tried to figure out what to wear. The jeans were out of the question. Covered in blood. As was the T-shirt and the tuxedo jacket. I was going to have to make another dumpster stop to get rid of them. I put on the tuxedo pants and one of Franklin's dress shirts—hopefully one he didn't much like. My Reeboks had a few bloodstains on them, but I didn't have any choice but to wear them. I put the bloody clothes in a shopping bag and went out to the living room.

Brian sat on the sofa staring at the TV as though it was on. He looked terribly sad.

"Where's Terry?"

"I don't know. He probably went to see his friend Cherry."

"Give me your clothes."

"What?"

"There's blood on your clothes. We need to get rid of them."

He stood up and peeled off the pink shorts and blue shirt he wore. There was blood on his arms and legs.

"You need to take a shower," I said, as I put his clothes into the bag.

"When you were gone before. I couldn't stand it." I'd spent a year in a transient hotel, working at a sleazy bar and not seeing anyone I knew. "I always want to know where you are. Promise me, Nick."

"You might have to lie to people. If they ask about me."

He shrugged. "So I'll lie."

We stood there awkwardly for a moment. Then he put his arms around me and hugged me tightly. He was crying now. Softly. My own eyes were tearing up.

"Thank you for saving me," he whispered into my ear.

That was a little hard to take. Sure, I saved him, but it was my fault he'd been kidnapped so I felt a little weird taking credit for it. I pulled away from him, saying, "I should go now. You should be okay, but be careful. Don't do anything foolish. Make up with your boyfriend. He's right, you know."

Brian wiped his face on his sleeve. I left him standing there in a pair of bikini briefs struggling not to cry. My own eyes stung as I went out the back door and down to the alley. I had no idea where I was going.

I drove around for a while looking for a place to dump the

bloody clothes. I put them in a dumpster behind a White Hen in Uptown. Then I drove over to Thorek.

It was nearly eleven, I think. Visiting hours had been over for a long time. I found the double doors to Intensive Care. I breezed right through. The unit was six rooms surrounding a large nursing station staffed with three nurses. I ignored them and peeked into rooms until I found Ross. The head of his bed had been raised. There were tubes going into his mouth, taped in place with white surgical tape. A machine was breathing for him. Every time it filled his lungs with air he seemed to jump a little bit. His eyes were closed.

I moved a chair over from the wall and sat by the bed. I wasn't there very long when a nurse came into the room. She didn't say anything to me. Just took Ross' pulse and then checked his IV. Before she walked out, she said to me, "Don't stay too long."

I took Ross' hand in mine. It felt dry and papery. I didn't say anything for a long time. And then, I told him everything. Everything that had happened that week and what I was going to do about it all. I wasn't sure he could hear me. Without thinking about it, I'd matched my breathing to the machine breathing for him. I'd begun to feel light-headed.

Ross wouldn't be alive much longer. That was clear. He was going to die. I'd known it for a long time, but it wasn't something I wanted to face. That was silly I suppose. There are many sorts of death and we face them all the time. Death happens all around us, every day, every hour, every minute. Time itself is a sort of death. A minute ends and will never return. Nor an hour. Or a day.

We are all yoked to time. I sat next to my dear friend wishing there was a way we could undo that yoke. That we could exist outside of time, together. The minutes died, one after another until finally I stood up, kissed Ross on his forehead, and said, "Good journey, my love." I can't be sure, but I think he squeezed my hand.

I like to think he did.

"SORRY TO BOTHER YOU LIKE THIS—" I said, standing at Clementine's door.

"No, it's all right," she said. She wore a pair of thin cotton summer pajamas, the kind with shorts. "Is something wrong? What happened with the police?"

"That was kind of a misunderstanding. I can't talk about it right now. The thing is, I know I just signed a lease, but I'm leaving town. I can write you a check for maybe three months, would that work?"

"Don't worry about it. I'll have the apartment rented in a month or so. The owners don't pay close attention. I'll just lose your lease."

"I'm not taking my stuff, so if you want just give it all away. There's nothing really—"

"I'll have it all moved down to storage. Just let me know if you want it sent somewhere."

I wouldn't. I knew I wouldn't. But she was being kind so I didn't say no. It felt wrong to reject her kindness.

"Clem?" a woman said from within the apartment. Clementine blushed. I hadn't realized... I winked at her and said, "Go back to bed."

Before I could walk away, she said, "Nick, take care of yourself."

"Yeah, I think I'll give that a try."

A few minutes later, I stood in front of the building looking up at my apartment. I asked myself again if there was anything up there I wanted, but there wasn't. The only thing I had in the world that meant anything to me were memories, and those I'd already packed.

Life is a shit sandwich. Two pieces of shit, but between them the most amazing filling, delicious, a taste so wonderful it electrifies your entire body and barely seems real. A filling that inspires us to keep chewing through the worst, hoping to get to that amazing center again. Yes, some of us get a lot more yummy goodness than others, but none of us forgets the deliciousness long enough to stop trying to chomp through the shit.

Honestly, I'd say I've been lucky. I'd loved three men and made a few good friends. I'd even managed to find a little bit of justice in a world that doesn't favor justice. I knew, though, if I stayed in Chicago there wouldn't be much of that amazing filling left. Or if I'd ever find it again. It was time to leave. I was done with the city or it was done with me. I didn't know which and it didn't even matter.

I'd parked Harker's Lincoln in the circular drive in front of the building. Just about in the spot where I'd been shoved into the back of a squad. I got in and drove out to Lake Shore Drive fully aware it was for the last time. I took the freeway south and out of Chicago.

As I drove, I couldn't help wondering what would happen now that I was gone. I wasn't entirely sure, but I had the feeling Deanna Hansen was on the hook for my full million-dollar bond. Owen would probably scramble to get the charges dropped—even without my being there. But if he didn't, then she'd owe the full amount. Rita Lindquist would be hanging around Chicago looking for me—making it more likely she'd get caught. And ASA Sanchez wouldn't be getting—that's when I had an idea. An interesting one.

Come Monday morning, I'd put in a call to Sanchez from a pay phone somewhere. I'd let her know I was gone, but had a parting gift for her. Something she wanted; a lot. Dresden. Deanna had said she wanted to buy the club and was willing to do just about anything to get it, and that included coercion, intimidation and threats. I didn't want to wear a wire, but Jonathon Lidell might.

Yes, he might end up in the Chicago River, but I had a feeling Sanchez would put a lot more effort into protecting him than she would me. A local businessman made a much better witness than a dubious private investigator. He'd make an excellent witness and Sanchez couldn't just toss him aside the minute she got her tape—as I'm pretty sure she would have with me.

Maybe I was fooling myself. Maybe Lidell would be just as

likely to end up dead. But that would be his choice. He'd have a chance to save his business if he was willing to take the risk. He'd have a way to fight back. Sanchez would get what she wanted and Deanna would be screwed.

I just might do it.

I tried to avoid thinking about what would happen to my friends, but I couldn't help it. Rita would probably watch them for a while, looking for me. I wouldn't be there, so eventually she'd give up. She'd either get caught by the CPD or wander off to some other city. Then the lives of my friends, Brian and Franklin, Sugar, Terry, and for his last few days Ross, would return to what they were meant to be. Lives of happiness and tragedy, joy and sorrow, but without the danger and violence I brought.

Forty-five minutes later, at South Holland, I got off the highway and looked for a gas station. When I found one, I went inside and bought a map of Illinois. I figured it was one of many maps I'd buy.

Studying the map, I leaned against the car. In a few minutes, I'd get back on the 94 and take it until it connected with Interstate 80. When I got there I was going to have to either turn west or east. But I had no idea which way I wanted to go. East or west? I had no real preference, didn't know enough about either to choose. Didn't know where I might stop once I'd picked a direction.

After a deep breath, I reached into my pocket and pulled out a quarter. Took a good look at it. Washington's profile. 1973. Heads I'd go east, tails I'd go west. I balanced the quarter on my thumb and flicked it into the air.

It spun and spun and spun.

End Note

Well, it's been a long journey. More than a decade. Like writers everywhere I've been enormously helped by the people in my life. I hope I've done a good job of thanking them in the acknowledgments, but suspect I have not. I would like to single out my longtime editor, Joan Martinelli, who in addition to being quietly brilliant is also a wonderful friend. Those of us who have gotten to know her have been blessed.

I also want to say that while preparing this book, I decided to title it *Boystown 13: Fade Out* as both an homage to the great Joseph Hansen's first Dave Brandstetter book *Fadeout* and as a reference to my background as a screenwriter—I use the education I received at UCLA film school in my writing every day.

A big thank you to everyone who has enjoyed the series and stuck with it. You are the making of me.

Aunt Belle's Time Travel & Collectibles

Masc

Never Rest

Code Name: Liberty

About the Author

Marshall Thornton writes two popular mystery series, the *Boystown Mysteries* and the *Pinx Video Mysteries*. He has won the Lambda Award for Gay Mystery three times. His romantic comedy, *Femme* was also a 2016 Lambda finalist for Best Gay Romance. Other books include *My Favorite Uncle*, *The Ghost Slept Over* and *Masc*, the sequel to *Femme*. He is a member of Mystery Writers of America.

Manufactured by Amazon.ca
Bolton, ON

23601425R00122